to love a
KNIGHT

WAYNE JORDAN

KIMANI
ROMANCE

 KIMANI PRESS™

ISBN-13: 978-0-373-86043-2
ISBN-10:   0-373-86043-9

TO LOVE A KNIGHT

Copyright © 2007 by Wayne Jordan

www.kimanipress.com

Printed in U.S.A.

He stood inside the door, barely visible in the shadow.

Tamara suppressed an overwhelming urge to move closer, so she could see him more clearly.

"Now that you've seen that I'm fine, you can go," he said.

He was about to close the door when she stretched her hand out to stop it. "No need to be rude. I was just doing the neighborly thing. I'm assuming from the noise I heard and the way you're standing that you fell. I'm a doctor, so I'd like to make sure you're okay. Where's the living room?"

He didn't answer, but he pointed to the left. She tugged on his hand, willing him to follow her. He hesitated briefly, and then did.

When they reached the living room, he stopped her, extending his hand to turn on the lights in the dark room.

Tamara stood silently. It might not have been obvious to the average onlooker, but she immediately realized something about her neighbor as he stood before her clothed in only loose-fitting sleep pants.

The man was blind. He was also drop-dead gorgeous....

Books by Wayne Jordan

Kimani Romance

Embracing the Moonlight
One Gentle Knight
To Love a Knight

WAYNE JORDAN

lives on the beautiful tropical island of Barbados, where he's a high school teacher who writes romance. Since joining the ranks of those who are published, he's had people constantly ask him why he writes romance. The answer is simple. Writing romance seems as natural to him as breathing. Not that he started out wanting to be a romance author. He had dreams of being the next great Caribbean writer, and then he discovered popular fiction and found himself transported to strange but exciting worlds that he longed to visit. Since he was a voracious reader, he read for every genre, but romance became the genre that best allowed him to escape the crazy world we live in. He writes to make people "laugh and cry and laugh again," and if he succeeds in doing this, then he knows he's done a good job.

Dear Reader,

I'd like to wish all of you a Merry Christmas. When I conceptualized *To Love a Knight*, thoughts of Christmas were far from my mind. When my editor asked me to give the story a Christmas theme, I thought long and hard about Tamara Knight's story. Of course, she has grown up a bit, since this story takes place about five years after *One Gentle Knight*. And then I thought about the kind of man I'd want for her and knew he had to be special. So Kyle Austin, former cricketer, started to speak to me. Unfortunately, his first words were, "Bah, humbug!" Kyle hated Christmas and...he was blind.

By the end of the first chapter I found myself engrossed in telling this inspiring story. With its tortured hero and feisty heroine, I knew *To Love a Knight* would be something special.

I hope you enjoy *To Love a Knight*, and visiting Barbados again. By the time you read this, Russell's story will be done. For those who have read *One Gentle Knight*, I hope you were as intrigued as I am with George, Troy and Sandra. They are starting to talk to me and I'm totally enthralled.

I've also started to work on Daniel Buchanan's story, *Chasing Rainbows,* for those of you who keep asking.

I'd like to thank all my readers for your wonderful support and wish that you continue to enjoy the stories I write. Write me at author@waynejordan.com or visit my Web site at www.waynejordan.com.

Blessings,

Wayne J

To my brothers and sisters: Rawle, Paula, Mark,
Joy, Keisha and Khaj.
I hope each of you have discovered the joy of reading.

And to my cousin and friend Joanne,
who actually reads more than I do.

Prologue

The music pounded in his head, but all Kyle Austin could think of was the magic being worked on him. He groaned, his body tensing, aching for release, but he willed it under control. He had long reached the conclusion that his fiancée, Chantal, practiced witchcraft and knew exactly how to bring him to his knees.

Kyle's body tensed again. This time, the muscles in his stomach contracted, his back stiffening with the exertion.

He could wait no longer. He ached for the pleasure of release. He tensed for the final time, pumping faster as her legs wrapped tighter around him.

When Chantal groaned his name out loud, he stroked her one final time before his body trembled and spasm after spasm racked him.

Sweet heaven.

He never ceased to be amazed at the magic Chantal worked on every inch of his body. The things she could do with her lips, tongue, hands, toes... She knew exactly how to make him vulnerable and wanting. He didn't love her, and she knew it. But he wanted her enough to marry her.

And if sex like this was a prerequisite for happily ever after, Chantal was the perfect candidate to be his wife.

Kyle eased off her and pulled his pants up, no mean feat in the moving limousine. His clumsy attempts to right his appearance soon had Chantal laughing hysterically.

Of course, they would make love later, but once he'd entered the vehicle, he wanted her. He'd been unable to wait until they'd arrived home.

Now dressed, he glanced over at Chantal. She lay naked, her legs spread provocatively.

"Come here," he ordered.

Without hesitation, she came to him and sat on his lap, her full breasts firm with anticipation. He placed his mouth on one dusky nipple, suckling it and loving the taste of her. She held his head and drew him even closer until he felt he would drown in her scent.

He continued to suckle, enjoying the way she moaned and groaned against him. He would never grow tired of her. And thank goodness, she was as sex-crazy as he was.

And then the unexpected happened. The limousine swerved abruptly and his body slammed against the side. The last thing he remembered was Chantal's high-pitched scream, a flash of blinding light, and then darkness.

The Present

"He said that Christmas was a humbug, as I live!" cried Scrooge's nephew. "He believed it, too."

Charles Dickens,
A Christmas Carol

Chapter 1

Kyle Austin closed the door behind him, cautiously feeling his way across the room. When he reached the window he opened it, enjoying the feel of the cool breeze against his face.

December 10.

It was his birthday, but he felt no joy at the prospect of having lived another year. Instead, the day brought memories of a time he preferred not to remember. A day he tried to forget, but one that reared its ugly head each time the bold stench of Christmas filled the air.

It annoyed him.

Not that most things didn't annoy him these

days, but this was definitely his least favorite time of the year.

Christmas.

Kyle felt the sudden urge to say, "Bah, humbug," but decided against it. Christmas was two weeks away and he couldn't wait until it was over. Good thing he wasn't a radio or television buff. He preferred to spin one of his treasured vinyl singles on his antique record player to pass the time. Unfortunately, from the beginning of December until just after Christmas, the music of the season would saturate the island with its message of love and good cheer. He couldn't escape it and didn't like it one bit.

His "Bah, humbug" echoed in the room. There, he'd said it and he felt as delighted to say it as the character whose words Dickens had made famous.

Let the masses spread their commercial and religious propaganda under the guise of celebrating the Christ child's birth. He had no time for it. December 25 was just like any other day to him. He'd get up, dictate the latest chapter of his book and spend the rest of the day listening to music.

That was his daily routine. His daily monotonous routine.

But he had to be content. There was nothing else he could do. Not since his life had changed and he'd made the choice to live the life of a recluse.

The once-famous Kyle Austin, voted most valuable player, had been reduced to a dull shadow of his former self.

Once, Kyle had been surrounded by some of the most beautiful women in Barbados. He'd dated a Miss Barbados, a well-known local actress and an international singing starlet. Living his life in the spotlight, he'd basked in the adoring glow of women and his fans.

Until that Christmas five years ago when his life had changed forever. The day he'd almost lost his life.

Inevitably, for a while he'd continued to be in the public's eye and the reporters had pounced on his misfortune. Strange enough, they had always been vultures, but they had made him the darling of Barbadian newspapers.

After the accident, he'd just wanted to wallow in self-pity. There were times he'd wished he had died.

So Kyle had done the only thing he could do. He had withdrawn from society and tried to disappear. Fortunately, it had been easier than he had thought. But after a while, another sensational story had come along. Soon he'd become just a memory.

So here he was five years later, alone, with the exception of his live-in assistant who he paid handsomely to take care of him. Since Kyle lived near the university, Jared, a graduate student in psychology, had seemed the perfect candidate for the job.

At the time of the accident, his doctor had recommended that Kyle learn to cope on his own. But why should he when he had enough money to get someone to take care of him for the rest of his life? Combined with his savings from being one of the West Indies' best cricketers, the settlement from his accident had made Kyle a very wealthy man. But all the money in the world couldn't bring back what he'd lost. Sometimes he felt like a hollow shell, cracked and ready to shatter. Even so, he was determined to survive.

One thing he did know was that he didn't need anyone. He didn't even want a woman. Ironic, how a man who'd been so obsessed with the pleasures of sex could lose his appetite for something he'd once considered so essential.

When Chantal had finally walked out on him a few months after the accident, he had discovered a part of him that he'd never realized existed. He'd been slowly falling in love with her. Chantal's rejection had hurt more than he'd anticipated, but his inability to give her the lifestyle she'd grown accustomed to had made her departure inevitable.

Kyle had finally discovered that the men and women who fluttered around him like butterflies had only been using him. That realization had left a bitter taste in his mouth.

Five years later, he'd settled into a predictable routine. But it was at this time of year that he most felt all he had lost. The holiday seemed to mock him with its claim of "Joy to the World" and "Peace to All Men."

Kyle Austin felt no joy or peace. Neither did he feel any joy that it was his birthday.

The two events were mutually exclusive and he'd resolved long ago not to celebrate either.

He turned from the window, making his way toward the chair next to the radio. Sitting, he reached over, easily finding and pressing the pre-set channel.

The voice of his favorite cricket commentator came over the airwaves.

The latest match in the current series of one-day matches had already started. Today, he could listen to the game on the radio, but it had taken him two years to face the reality that he would never play again.

Now, he could listen, stifling the envy he still felt each time the team had a series of matches.

He'd loved the game. Still loved it. He'd wanted to be like the greats, Sir Garfield Sobers or Brian Lara.

Sometimes in the silence of the night, he could

still hear the roaring of the crowds and feel the smoothness of his bat in his hands. Batting was a dance, poetry in motion, and inside he ached for that beauty again.

Instead, his life was a stagnant pool of nothingness. All the things he'd brushed aside in the wild, crazy days before the accident now defined his very existence.

He wondered for the hundredth time about the insensitivity of life.

What would become of him?

Maybe this would be the rest of his life. He knew he wasn't happy, but he didn't want to be part of the world he had once belonged to. He couldn't endure the grim pity or platitudes that everyone seemed to think were necessary.

He sighed, turning the radio off.

The West Indian cricket team had won again.

But how could he celebrate when all he could feel was sadness for the life he had lost?

Tamara Knight put the phone down and sighed. She loved her brother Shayne, but he was beginning to annoy her with his constant calls. She knew he was worried about her and she was grateful that he'd found this place for her, but she wished he'd remember that she was no longer a bright-eyed university student.

She was a woman! And she was also a veterinary doctor.

At twenty-five, she was capable of taking care of herself. She was one year out of veterinary school, had recently completed an internship with Doctor Boyce and she was finally ready to begin her own life. The doors of Tamara's Ark would be opening officially the day after New Year's.

For now she intended to enjoy her favorite time of year. Christmas. Of course, she had Gladys to thank for all her happy Christmas memories. Her older brother, Shayne, had not been one for big Christmas celebrations while she was growing up. He'd been too busy with his work on the plantation, but Gladys, their housekeeper, had made sure that the plantation house wafted with the delicious aroma of baked ham, fruitcake and the spiciness of sorrel punch. No one could make the local drink like Gladys did.

Later in the week she planned to go into Bridgetown and get a Christmas tree for her new place. Russell, her twin brother, had promised to help her get it home. In turn, Tamara had promised to help decorate the enormous tree which would grace their family room.

Home.

She should be saying her former home, she thought.

She'd finally moved out two months ago. She'd spent most of those months overseeing the finishing touches to the building which would house her new practice.

Tamara looked around her office, feeling an overwhelming pride at what she'd achieved. She was proud of what she'd done with her inheritance. Her parents had left a legacy to each of their three children. She'd used hers to create Tamara's Ark.

She'd worked hard to achieve what she wanted. That was because her big brother Shayne had instilled in his siblings a respect for hard work and accomplishment. Both she and Russell had received scholarships to attend university. She'd graduated top of her class and had won several awards during her years of study.

But that was all in the past.

She intended to spend the next few weeks preparing for her grand opening and filling her new home with the spirit of Christmas.

Now, however, she was going into the stable to see her two horses, Storm and Thunder, and Princess, her dog. She couldn't wait to see Princess's pups again. They were so adorable.

She exited her office at the side of the building and headed to the stable at the back of the compound.

When Tamara entered the stable a few minutes later, Storm reared his head. His eyes bright with excitement, he ambled towards her. Thunder remained still, her eyes wary. The mare had not grown accustomed to the move yet, and each time Tamara came to visit, she sensed the horse's disapproval and confusion.

When Tamara reached them, she dug into the pocket of her jeans, taking out the two apples she'd brought for them.

Storm nodded his thanks before gently taking the apple in his mouth to crunch on it. Thunder moved cautiously toward them, hesitating before she took the apple from Tamara's hand.

As the horse ate, Tamara touched her side. Thunder was pregnant again. Of course, she'd promised this foal to Darius. She smiled, thinking of her nephew. He'd just started school and delighted in reciting his alphabets to her whenever she went over to the plantation house.

Darius was a bundle of energy. She was still amazed at how he'd grown. Born prematurely at twenty-eight weeks, his first few months had been a period of uncertainty for the whole family. Now he was a healthy, intelligent boy. And Tamara loved him as much as she loved the other members of her family.

She thought of Carla, the woman who'd given her brother love and happiness. Of course, the fact that her sister-in-law was a romance reader and they now split the cost of their monthly treasures from the local bookstores, only served to cement the respect they had for each other.

Tamara wondered if she'd ever find a love like Carla and Shayne shared. After five years, Shayne and Carla still behaved like they were on their honeymoon. At times, she caught Carla staring at Shayne with dreamy eyes and she wished for that same thing for herself.

However, there was no time for that. Until she'd built her business and had enough clients, she would simply have no time for a real relationship. She would have to be satisfied with fantasizing about the sexy alpha heroes of her favorite romance novels.

Patting both of the horses, she headed farther into the stable. Princess lay with her pups in the same box Tamara had provided for them a few weeks before. Princess, who had come through the birth wonderfully, looked positively regal as a new mother.

She barked softly in welcome as the four pups attached to her nipples suckled peacefully.

For a while, Tamara stood there watching the domestic scene. Eventually the puppies pulled away and started to play. They were growing quickly and had already begun to frolic around the stable. Though she'd fallen in love with each of them, she knew she'd soon have to part with them.

For a while she played with the pups, giggling

at their antics, but eventually they collapsed in exhaustion and slept quietly.

As Tamara made her way back to her apartment within the compound, her eyes were drawn to the house next door. She'd caught glimpses of the two men who lived there on several occasions. She regularly saw the younger one leave during the day. He usually wore a backpack, and Tamara guessed he was a student.

The other man intrigued her. He rarely left the house. When he did venture outside, it was always at nighttime. He would sit on the patio. Unfortunately, on those rare occasions, she still hadn't seen much of him. The houses were too far apart for her to see his face clearly.

She couldn't help being curious about her mystery neighbor.

Someday, she decided, she was going to meet him. There was something about him that intrigued her.

That night, Jared informed Kyle he was going to a party and would be out late. Since Jared rarely went out, Kyle was glad to see him take a night off from studying. When Jared left that evening, Kyle made sure he was in his bedroom. He didn't want Jared to worry about him. Kyle wanted the younger man to go out and have a good time for a change.

Of course, Kyle didn't go to sleep. It was way before his usual bedtime, so he lay down listening to a call-in radio program.

When the program was over, Kyle slipped from his bed, took his clothes off and headed for the shower.

Completing the task in record time, he dried his body and found the track pants he liked to sleep in. Reaching for his MP3 player, he realized it was not where he usually kept it.

He must have left it downstairs.

He sighed. He left the room and headed down the stairs. Halfway down, however, he felt his feet give way, and he slammed onto the steps. His body rolled down the remainder, despite his attempt to break the momentum of his fall.

At the bottom of the staircase, he remained still. His body ached, but after a thorough probe, he realized that nothing was broken.

He reached out, feeling for the steps, and began the painful process of pulling himself up.

And then he heard a voice to his left, in the direction of the front door.

"Hello? Is someone in there? I heard a noise."

At first he decided not to answer, but when the voice persisted, he reluctantly said, "Everything is all right."

"If you say so, but I'm not leaving here until I

find out what's going on. I was jogging by when I heard the noise."

Reluctantly, he moved toward the entrance, slid the bolt and opened the door.

A man stood inside, the light behind him casting a dull shadow across the threshold, so she couldn't see his face clearly. Her first impression of him was that he was tall—very tall—and a mass of muscle, with broad shoulders.

Tamara suppressed an overwhelming urge to move closer, so she could see him more clearly. She decided it was best to exercise some semblance of decorum. She stepped back.

For what seemed like hours they continued to stare at each other.

"Good. So now you've seen that I'm fine, can I go get some rest? You've done your good deed for the day."

He was about to close the door when she stretched her hand out to stop it. "No need to be sarcastic and rude. Just doing the neighborly thing. Maybe if you'd fallen on your higher-than-mighty ass, you'd be a lot more polite. However, since I'm a doctor and qualified to evaluate you, I would still prefer to check and see if something is wrong. I'm assuming from the noise I heard and by the way you're standing that you fell." She tried to keep the laughter from her voice. Not that she cared much. He seemed like a really snotty individual.

He lowered his head and Tamara wondered if he was embarrassed, but he raised it immediately and gave her a hard, menacing scowl. Nonplussed, she took his hand and said, "Come, no need to be difficult. I'm telling you, I'm a doctor. Well, a vet, but you might as well let me check and see that nothing is wrong with you. Where's the living room?"

She tugged his hand and then stopped. "Where are the lights? It's a bit too dark in here for my liking."

When he didn't answer, she felt around for a switch by the door, and pressed it. Nothing happened.

"You really need to put a light in here. No wonder you fell. Where's the living room? The kitchen?"

When he pointed to the left, she tugged on his hand again, willing him to come with her. He hesitated briefly, but followed.

Good. He was moving reluctantly, but at least he was moving. She had no intention of leaving him until she knew he was fine.

When they finally reached the room, he stopped. Then he extended his hand and switched the lights on.

Tamara stood silently. It wouldn't have been so

obvious to the average onlooker, but she realized something about her neighbor as he stood before her, clothed only in loose-fitting track pants.

He was blind.

At the same time recognition dawned. Her mystery neighbor was Kyle Austin, the famous cricketer who'd disappeared after the accident that had almost killed him a few years ago.

Not only were his eyes vacant, but a puckered scar ran along the right side of his face.

Tamara Knight, veterinarian, Barbadian scholar and modern woman, felt a hot compassion for this man that tore right through her heart.

"Come," Kyle heard her say. "Sit here in this chair and I'll see if anything serious is wrong."

He let her lead him to the chair he knew was to the left of the television and he sat down on it.

She knew. He'd felt her hesitation. Her uncertainty about what to say or do.

"I can take care of myself, you know," he said.

"I'm sure you can, but I won't sleep well if I don't check to see if you're hurt."

So he decided to sit and subject himself to what seemed like an inevitable intrusion.

She touched and prodded and probed and then something happened. Kyle became totally aware of her.

Her touch was soft, a whisper of skin on his skin, a gentle caress. And her scent. Healthy and fresh. She'd been running. He could tell that much. Jared had mentioned the woman who lived next door. Not that he'd been interested, but his curiosity had piqued a bit when Jared had told him that the vet who'd moved in was beautiful and sexy.

He wished he could see her. He liked her voice. A husky, seductive tone that would make a man ache to be in her bed.

Definitely sexy.

"So, what's the verdict, Dr. Vet?"

"You can call me Tamara. And it seems that you'll be fine, but you need to be a lot more careful. You could have broken your neck."

"I'll be fine. I'm accustomed to taking care of myself. It was only a little fall."

"Where's your friend?" she asked.

"He's gone to a party."

"You need someone to take care of you when he's not here. Or a guide dog. That would help to avoid these little accidents."

"No," he almost shouted.

He was surprised when she did not respond. His respect for her went up a notch, but she was still annoying.

"I think it's about time I get up to bed. I've taken up too much of your time already."

"No invitation for coffee?" she whispered in that seductive voice that was working magic on him.

"Maybe another time. I'm a bit shaken from the accident," he said, his deep tones dripping with sarcasm. He heard her soft laughter. She knew he was lying.

"Oh, Mr. Austin, sorry to disappoint you, but I'll be back."

"And why would you want to do that?" he asked.

When her answer came, it was as unexpected as a hurricane in the month of December, and its impact was just as unsettling.

"I always try to be honest. So I'll tell you my reason." She paused as if for dramatic effect. "I fell in love with you tonight."

She didn't wait for his reaction. He heard her rise from where she knelt before him.

With a warm, husky laugh that worked its way up his spine, she said, "I'll see you tomorrow. I need to get home and take a shower. I have a lot of work to do tomorrow. Since you can take care of yourself, make sure you lock up properly. And try not to fall again. Next time, I might not be around to help you."

He laughed in response, but listened as her soft footsteps moved away from him.

He wanted to call her back, to find out what she meant by that ridiculous statement.

Fell in love.

She either had a great sense of humor or she was crazy. Maybe both.

Hours later, as he lay in bed, unable to sleep, he could still hear the echoes of her laughter.

Tamara closed the cupboard, placed the jar of coffee on the counter and unscrewed the lid. She didn't drink coffee often, but she needed a cup tonight.

Kyle Austin.

She had recognized him immediately. She'd been one of his greatest fans. She'd loved to watch him play and then he'd had the accident while she was overseas. Now here she was living next door to him.

When she'd gotten her first complete glimpse of him, she felt a pain so intense that she'd almost cried. She'd wanted to hug him and take the pain away. She could see it in his eyes, the hollow look of a man who no longer loved life. She remembered clearly the twinkle in his gorgeous bedroom eyes as he smiled from glossy tabloid pages. He'd always had some beautiful woman draped around him.

Like all the girls in her classes at the university, she'd had a serious crush on him and since she was a sports fan, she'd totally idolized him.

Now he was blind. She was surprised that he'd handled his situation by hiding away in the countryside. He'd always seemed so strong and sure of himself.

Tamara wondered how many people knew about his blindness. She couldn't remember hearing anything about it at the time of the accident.

She moved instinctively toward the small entertainment room she'd created for herself. A thirty-inch television beckoned her, but she felt no desire to watch a program. What drew her were the shelves and shelves of books she'd collected over the years. It had been a massive undertaking to move them here.

Of course, more than half of them were romance novels, an addiction that had begun the first time she'd held a book with a hero and heroine just like her on the cover. Over the years, she'd expanded her taste, reading novels of all genres and authors of all races.

On the top shelf were a few new ones her sister-in-law had given her. At almost eight months pregnant, Carla had spent most of her time reading, a hobby she totally enjoyed. After the premature birth of her first son, Darius, almost five years ago, neither she nor Shayne wanted to take the risk that anything could happen, so Carla had, without any argument, complied with the doctor's decision to rest as much as possible. Of course, resting was now synonymous with reading.

Tamara picked one of the new novels from the shelf and moved toward her bedroom at the back of the house.

Thirty minutes later, she closed the book and sighed with contentment. An image of Kyle, one that had been stuck in her head since the first time she saw him play in a game while she was still in high school, came to mind. It had been his debut match after he'd joined the team and made an excellent score. He'd been handsome and oh, so sexy.

Now, he was a pale shadow of his former self, but even so she liked what she had seen. Though he seemed bitter, he also appeared mature and she assumed that what he had been through was responsible for that change.

She'd been shocked by his face, and was glad he hadn't seen her expression. He couldn't be called handsome anymore. The scar was too distinct and raw, but it gave his face character. She was surprised to discover that she still found him so attractive.

She hadn't failed to see that he was still fit and she'd ached to touch him in a more intimate way. While he sat before her she couldn't help but see his well-toned chest covered with hair that made its way down his defined six-pack. The thin line had disappeared below his track pants.

She'd itched to touch him, but that would have

been inappropriate. And more importantly, she didn't want to scare him. She might privately dream about one day sharing his bed, but for now she was more concerned about his state of mind.

He seemed rather unschooled in what he needed to know to help him deal with his blindness. She hadn't seen a cane, or a guide dog, or anything.

It was as if he'd accepted his blindness as a part of who he was, without wanting to really live.

Men! They were so stubborn and caught up with the illusion of being macho. She'd seen the uncertainty on his face and knew he didn't want her there, but still…he intrigued her. She'd experienced a feeling that overwhelmed her when she'd knelt before him. She was realistic enough to know that love, true love, was not about meeting someone for the first time and feeling sorry for him. And yet…her feelings for him were genuine and her attraction to him electric. She had every intention of exploring the possibilities.

She had no reservations at all about his blindness or how he looked.

She would enjoy waking up next to him each morning, but she needed to find out what had happened to him during the last few years.

The Kyle Austin she'd seen on television had been a man who lived life to the fullest, and his only commitment seemed to be to cricket.

She wondered how much of the real man was still there. In any case, she had every intention of teaching him to live again.

After she helped him to heal, then there'd be time for love.

Chapter 2

The next morning, Kyle woke up feeling exhausted and grumpy. After the accident he'd found it difficult to sleep, frequently waking up just before sunrise to the sound of his own screams of pain. In the past year or so, he'd settled into a comfortable routine, and only on the rare occasion did the nightmares of that night resurface. But last night he'd hardly closed his eyes, and he knew exactly the cause of his restlessness.

Tamara.

During the night he'd experienced the strangest feeling. It was almost as if his body were coming alive. Her scent seemed to linger in the air, and he

could still feel the energy that had sparked between them.

As Kyle thought about her, he found himself
becoming erect, and felt that sweet, painful tension that craved release. But he called on years of
self-control since the accident to bring his body
under subjection. It had not been easy, but he'd
eventually learned to stifle his need for sex.

He must be going crazy. He was far from being
a poetic kind of person. Oh, he'd hated literature
at school. Those boring books that no one really
wanted to read, but were forced to in the name of
education. Fortunately, many of the books he had
to study had already been turned into movies. He'd
been able to get decent grades by watching videos
of the classics.

It was ironic that after years of having no
interest in reading, he'd had a measure of success
writing fiction for young adults.

He slipped from the bed, running his hand over
the clock on the bureau. Just after six. His usual
time to get up. Jared would already be gone on
his morning jog. The expected jolt of envy came,
but he preferred not to dwell on his inability to
engage in the activity. All those activities remained in his past.

He still got his exercise in the well-equipped

gym he'd had set up for his personal use. He'd go, have a good workout, have breakfast and then continue to work on his latest manuscript.

In the gym he followed his usual routine. Thirty minutes on the treadmill and thirty minutes on the bicycle. In the evening, when Jared returned from classes, they would work out together as they did each day.

He looked forward to this part of the day. He loved the sense of invincibility that came when he pushed himself to the limit. He didn't feel restricted by his lack of vision, but loved the power that came from making his body do whatever he wanted it to. In the gym he felt in control.

Last night, however, he'd definitely lost it. The feisty, annoying Tamara had made him feel vulnerable. She was the first person in a long time to make him feel naked and exposed.

When he'd turned the light on for her, he'd almost bolted. He couldn't stand to let her see him. Not that *he'd* ever seen what he looked like. He'd awakened from the coma in a world of darkness that terrified him, that still terrified him.

But he was sure it couldn't be pleasant. He'd touched the puckered, uneven scar on the left side of his face and knew he could no longer be called handsome.

He was the fairy-tale beast of the story, but he

had no time for fairy tales. His life was steeped in reality—the cold, hard reality that he was blind and ugly. No woman would want him. He was destined for a life of loneliness.

He'd learned his lesson with Chantal. All she'd had to offer him was pity…and then rejection. The love she'd professed had just been her love for the image—the man he'd once been.

Kyle Corey Austin.

Former world-class cricketer and now just a shell of his former self.

An hour later, he headed back to his room, taking a quick shower. While he was dressing, Jared knocked on his door.

"Kyle, I'm on my way out. I have a meeting with my thesis supervisor at nine. I'll be home early."

"Cool, I'll see you tonight."

After Jared had gone, he finished dressing. He then headed downstairs to the kitchen.

Since he didn't want to risk using the stove, he took a carton of juice from the refrigerator, poured a glass and decided to take in a game on the sports channel.

Reaching the living room, Kyle turned the television on and listened to the previous night's NBA game that he'd recorded.

Ms. Simpson would arrive soon and she'd prepare breakfast, do some cleaning and then cook dinner that he and Jared would share that evening.

He wondered what the alluring Tamara was doing. She was probably still sleeping, or getting breakfast, or maybe taking a shower.

In the midst of his musing, he heard a knock at the door. It couldn't be Ms. Simpson. She had her own key.

The postman? No, there was a mailbox.

He moved from the kitchen, walking toward the door.

The person knocked again, this time harder.

He opened the door and demanded angrily, "Who is it? Are you trying to knock my door off?"

There was silence and then husky laughter.

His heart raced. His body tingled.

"It's your friendly next-door neighbor," the voice came back at him. Soft and seductive. The same voice that had haunted his dreams.

He breathed deeply, and tried in vain to suppress the excitement he felt.

"I'm sorry to disturb you, but I made breakfast and made too much for myself, so I thought that the neighborly thing to do would be to share. Where is the kitchen?"

He turned his head, following her voice into the house.

She was pushy, wasn't she?

He pointed toward the corridor that led to the kitchen, and followed when her footsteps moved in that direction.

When she reached the kitchen, she said, "You can sit where you usually do. I'll just follow your lead. I don't want to move anything I shouldn't."

He heard the clink of plates and the rattle of utensils.

"Okay, I'm going to use the microwave to warm it up. But before I do, I should introduce myself properly. I'm Tamara Knight and I'm the island's newest vet. I moved in a few months ago and my practice opens in three weeks. Of course, I'm very excited. You must come over to play with my dog and her puppies. And I'll introduce you to my two horses, Storm and Thunder. How do you want your tea?"

He hoped she would give him time to answer. When she didn't continue to rattle on, he responded, "Two sugars, no milk."

"Good. Hope you like pancakes. I've also brought along some whole-wheat muffins. My brother Shayne loves them, and our housekeeper, Gladys, taught me how to make them so they're light and fluffy."

Her voice drew nearer. He waited as she placed breakfast on the table.

There was silence.

"So do you plan to sit there all morning and not eat? I got up early just to make breakfast for you."

"You did?"

"Okay, I'm stretching the truth a bit. I'm usually up at the stroke of five, jog for half an hour or so, have breakfast and then feed the animals. But I make up for it at night. I don't usually stay up past ten o'clock."

"Which means you're pretty fit?"

"Yes, definitely. I'm an exercise fanatic. I've ordered some equipment for a gym, but I prefer to run outdoors. There is nothing better than the wind blowing against a sweaty body. You should come and run with me sometime."

"No!" he barked at her.

"Oh, well. That's your choice," she said, seeming unfazed by his abrupt response.

"I don't go outside much," he said. He felt a need to lessen his rude response.

"Because you're blind?" Her voice was a whisper.

"Isn't it obvious?"

"Not really. I know blind people who work and jog and party."

"Well, more power to them. I'm happy with my life. I have no need for all that socializing."

"As I said, it's your choice. But you need to eat or I'm going to have to eat what I brought for you. I have a healthy appetite."

In response, he turned his head toward the table and wondered which appetite she meant.

"The plate's right before you. Pancakes at three o'clock, muffins at nine, bread at twelve. And hold this." She reached for his hand, placing a mug of tea in it.

"Thank you," he said.

For a while they ate in silence, something that surprised him. The occasional clink of the fork on her plate suggested that she was concentrating on her meal.

When he heard her fork land on the plate with a measure of finality, he smiled briefly in anticipation.

"So what are your plans for the day? I have so much to do. I'm working on getting my office organized."

"So you're opening your own practice? Jared told me he saw the announcement in the paper."

"Yeah, right next door."

"You must be excited."

"Yes, I definitely am. I've dreamt of this for years. I finished my internship a year ago, so now I can work on my own until I can afford to hire someone to help me. Hopefully, I can build a successful practice."

"I hope you've done some advertising?"

"Yes, I've taken care of all that. Of course, my brother Shayne believes he has to do everything for me. He has the plantation to run, so I insisted he let me do this on my own."

"Your brother owns a plantation?" He paused. "Your brother is Shayne Knight?"

"Yes, he's my big brother."

"I know him. We went to high school together. We weren't the best of friends, but I partied with him and his good friends a few times. What were their names, now?" He could see his classmates as clearly as if it were yesterday. "Yes, Troy and George."

"That's them. They are still the best of friends."

"They were the coolest at school." He stopped, unsure of raising the subject. "I was sorry to hear about your parents' death. I think I was in Australia on tour, but I'm sure I sent Shayne a card when I returned home."

"I have to let him know that I met you. Shayne's married now. To the nicest woman ever. They have a boy and Carla's pregnant with their second child. You must let me take you to visit them. Shayne will be glad to see you. He was one of your greatest fans." She stopped, and he realized why she had.

"It's okay, Tamara. I accepted a long time ago that I will never play cricket again."

"I'm sorry."

"I don't want your pity."

She was silent.

"Thanks for the breakfast," he said, rising abruptly from the chair. "I have to go up to my room and make a few phone calls. You can leave the things in the sink. My housekeeper will take care of that when she arrives. Let yourself out."

Kyle turned to move away when the softest of hands stopped him.

"I enjoyed having breakfast with you. We must do it again sometime soon."

He felt the tender whisper of her lips on his cheek, and then she was gone, her footsteps echoing in the hallway. The sound of the front door being closed brought him back to reality with a thud.

He noticed that he was trembling.

Her scent lingered, and he inhaled deeply.

What was happening to him? he wondered.

In just a few hours, Tamara Knight had entered his life and disrupted it. He had no need for her. He was happy with his life and now she was making him wish for things that he'd learned to live without.

She made him ache.

He ached for the scent and touch of a woman. She'd stirred parts of him that he'd thought were dead.

As Kyle stood, he became aware of his arousal. It was a throbbing painful reminder that a woman could still work her magic on him.

Oh, he was human and sometimes in the middle

of the night he'd awake erect, wishing for the soft body of a willing woman next to him, but he'd learned over the years how to deal with those times.

Now, in just a few short hours, his body had betrayed him once again.

Kyle left the kitchen, knowing that there was one way to deal with this problem.

He climbed the stairs, headed to his room, stripped his clothes off and walked directly to the bathroom. A good cold shower was the best way to cool the heat that raged inside his body.

He was infuriating!
He annoyed her!

Tamara slammed the door behind her. What was she going to do? She couldn't help thinking about him. He'd wormed his way into her system and whatever she did to stop it, his image continued to mock each of her attempts to erase him from her mind.

When she'd awakened that morning, Kyle had been the first person she thought of. Standing in the shower, she daydreamed of how it would be to have him standing next to her, tempting her with his gentle, husky voice.

She couldn't count the times during the night when the image of his rugged face had flashed before her eyes. She knew she already had it bad—

really bad—for him. Somehow Kyle Austin had given rise to feelings she didn't quite comprehend. She wasn't even sure if they were feelings she wanted. At this time in her life, falling in love was the last thing she needed to do. She didn't want love.

For the past few years, she'd focused on her education. Being a vet had been her childhood dream.

Now, the focus was on building her business and having enough clients to make Tamara's Ark successful. She wanted to make it work. She wanted to prove that despite being born well-off, she could be an independent and productive member of her community.

She rose from the chair where she sat, heading to the exit at the back of the house that led directly to the state-of-the-art facility that had been constructed to her specifications.

It was time to feed the animals. She needed to be with them. They were not like people, who were complicated and demanded so much from you or who could hurt you. They needed her.

As Tamara moved from the house, she thought of her first relationship.

In the end she'd been hurt beyond repair. At least, she'd thought so. Brian had been a slightly older classmate. She'd fallen for him hard. He'd made her feel like a woman for the first time in her young life. So much focus on schoolwork had left her lonely and aching for romance, so when Brian showed an interest in her, she'd been elated.

They'd become lovers and she'd been happy. Then one day, she'd overheard one of the students from his home island of St. Vincent wonder what Tamara would do when Brian returned to his *wife.*

She'd been devastated and she'd also been embarrassed to realize her fellow students knew that she was sleeping with a married man. She had immediately collected all her things from his room and returned to the dorm room she'd hardly ever used.

That night she'd cried herself to sleep and the next morning, she'd returned to her studies, refusing to have anything to do with him again. She'd thought it would be difficult since he was in most of her classes, but he'd made it easy. He had wasted no time in moving on to another naive young woman aching for affection.

Tamara pushed the door of the stable open and the spirited welcome from Storm eased her troubled thoughts. Thunder, lying on the ground, rose. The mare's welcome was as enthusiastic as the stallion's.

Tamara moved quickly toward them. She could tell they were hungry. Her visit to Kyle's home had delayed their morning meal and she quickly put out their feed. When they were happily eating, she moved toward Princess and her pups.

As usual, they were playing with each other. When they saw her, they looked up and raced toward her, stumbling and knocking each other over in their attempt to reach her.

Lowering herself to the ground, Tamara giggled as the pups jumped on her, fighting to find a comfortable spot in her lap. Soon they were licking her all over her face until she tumbled to the ground. The puppies scrambled all over her, barking with excitement.

Tamara remembered days like these when she was a child. She wished that she could bring those days back. When she didn't have a care in the world. That uncomplicated time before her parents' death.

She'd been devastated, but she'd never allowed her grief to show. Only Gladys had reached out to her in her time of despair. Shayne had tried, but as a young twenty-two-year-old bachelor he'd been unsure how to deal with a twelve-year-old on the verge of womanhood. Shayne had willingly placed her in Gladys's arms. But Tamara had understood. She knew Shayne loved her more than anything, and she loved him back equally. Back then, Shayne had definitely been dealing with his own pain. She remembered clearly the nights he had come home drunk and retired to his room. She even remembered the night her twin brother Russell had cussed Shayne out.

The next morning when Shayne had come downstairs, he'd told them he was taking over the running of the plantation and that they were now his responsibility.

Shayne had sacrificed so much for them. From that time, Tamara vowed never to let him down.

She hugged the lone puppy that sat in her arms. She would keep this one. She would have to find homes for the others because she simply could not keep them all.

She rose, placing the puppy next to his mother, while he looked at her with soulful eyes, as if begging her to stay.

He barked, running toward her.

"In a week or so, I'll let you come with me," she said to him, bending to tickle him behind the ears.

He looked up at her as if he understood every word she had said, wagged his tail and walked back to his mother, where he placed himself firmly on one teat and began to suckle.

Tamara turned away. She needed to get back to the house. She still had lots of calls to make to ensure that all her equipment and supplies would arrive before she opened in three weeks, just after the New Year. Tamara figured if she did most of the preparation for the opening now, she would be able to relax for the rest of the holiday season. She intended to enjoy Christmastime.

She just loved Christmas.

And, Tamara vowed to make sure her neighbor Kyle Austin enjoyed his Christmas as well. He didn't seem to have anyone besides his housemate and his housekeeper to celebrate with. So Tamara took it on herself to make his holiday merry. Thinking of him sitting alone in that house all day strengthened her determination. She definitely needed to give him some Christmas cheer.

As she drew near to the house, she heard the sharp shrill of her telephone.

Good, she was expecting an important call. Right now, she needed to take care of business. She'd put Kyle Austin at the back of her mind for as long as it took her to square away the details of opening her office.

Once she'd done that…all bets were off!

"Mr. Austin, I leavin'. Jared just pulled up. I goin' see you tomorrow mornin' as usual, but remember tomorrow is supermarket day, so I goin' to be a bit late."

"I remember, Ms. Simpson. I'll be fine until you get here."

"Good, I don't like leavin' you alone too long."

"I'll be fine."

"You have a good afternoon," she said.

"I will."

Her footsteps made a sharp staccato as she moved down the hallway. Ms. Simpson did everything as if it were the last thing she had to do before she expired, but he loved her energy and she took good care of him.

Kyle heard Jared's voice and knew Ms. Simpson had stopped him. Of course, along with her energy, the housekeeper loved to talk. At times, he had to lock himself in the den. At least she knew that when he was there, he did not want to be disturbed.

Fifteen minutes later, Jared entered the room.

"Evening, Kyle," he said, his voice filled with laughter. "Sorry it took me so long to get here. Ms. Simpson kept me a bit, as usual, but she means well. You ready to start work?"

"Yes, definitely. I want to get the final chapter finished today. My editor wants the book no later than February, but we're near the end."

"She will be delighted. Since your first book sold so well, I'm sure that she has high expectations for this one."

"Yes, I still can't believe that it did so well. She's still trying to get me to reveal who I am, but I refused again. She thinks it will increase sales. But what would people think if they found out Kyle Austin wrote children's books?"

"Not children's books—adventure stories for boys. What's wrong with that?" Jared questioned.

"I'm not saying that there's anything wrong with it, but it's not something that people would expect me to do."

"Well, the choice is ultimately yours. I'll go transcribe what you dictated over the weekend and set up the equipment for you to get started on the next chapter."

"Thanks. I don't know what I'd do without you."

"Oh, you'd just find another university student to work for you."

"I hear you. I may not be the most sensitive individual, but I'm glad you're working with me."

There was silence. Kyle sensed that Jared was at a loss for words. In the years they'd worked together, Kyle had never thought it necessary to say much about the good work Jared was doing. Kyle paid him well and as far as he was concerned that was enough.

When Jared didn't answer, Kyle was sure that his assistant had passed out in shock.

When he spoke, he asked, "Are you all right, boss?"

"I'm fine," Kyle replied. "But let's not dwell too much on this moment."

"Cool, I'll go set up the equipment before something even stranger takes place." And then he walked away, his laughter another strange and unfamiliar sound to Kyle.

What the hell was happening?

Something strange was in the air.

Kyle knew exactly who'd caused it.

His next-door neighbor.

He didn't even want to say her name. Tamara was wreaking havoc with his mind. And it was as if she had sprinkled some magic dust in his house.

He didn't like it one bit. She'd touched him in a strange way. Making him think of crazy, fanciful things, making him dream of her lying next to him in bed and the two of them making wild passionate love.

And he didn't want it.

He rose, making his way to his office. He knew his way by memory. At the end of the hallway, turn left, and then take twenty-five steps and he'd be right there.

He gripped the frame of the entrance and stepped into the room, the clicking of the computer a swift comforting noise.

The clicking stopped. "Everything is set up in the other room," Jared said. "If you need me, just press the buzzer. I'll have the headphones on."

"Thanks," Kyle replied, moving toward the connecting room.

Sitting in his usual chair, he placed the wireless mike and headphones on his head and started speaking.

For a while, he weaved the final chapter of his story. It was a tale about a boy, not born to be a hero, finding himself in a world where good and evil battled. The child had to draw on his inner strength to defeat the evil forces.

When Kyle spoke the words "The End," he sighed in relief. He knew this story was better than his first. His protagonist had grown, had become the hero Kyle wanted him to be.

Kyle sighed at the irony of it all. He remembered weaving these stories as a teenager in school. His writing teacher had always told him he was good, but he had frowned at doing any kind of schoolwork, and had done just enough to get by. He hadn't wanted to be called a sissy, so studying had been way down on his agenda.

He was a man and taking part in a man's sport was important. He'd been good at soccer, but cricket, the sport rooted in the island's colonial past, had enchanted him with its flow and rhythm.

At times like these, he remembered the cheering of the crowd when he walked onto the field, his bat raised in the air, embracing the energy of the fans that helped him to play at his best. And he'd played to the crowd, giving them what they wanted, using his skill and natural talent to mesmerize them with his magic.

Cricket had made him a star and women had loved him for his prowess both on and off the field.

He remembered the woman who'd introduced him to the joys of sex just after he'd made his debut appearance for the West Indies team at twenty-one. He'd been a shy young man and totally inexperienced. She'd taken him under her wing and taught him all he needed to know, until he was so comfortable in his own skin, he'd moved on to other willing bodies. Young women with firm breasts and long legs that spread at the touch of his hands.

There had been no turning back.

He hadn't been promiscuous. He'd chosen his women well and most of his affairs lasted for quite a few months, but he'd absolutely avoided commitment.

Now here he was, a crippled, dried-up remnant of who he'd once been. And for the first time in a long time, Kyle wondered if his self-imposed exile, his life of seclusion, was really what he wanted.

He rose from his seat and retreated to the safety of his room.

He heard no clicking. Instead he heard Jared's voice like a chill in the air.

He was singing a Christmas carol.

And like a bucket of water, Kyle remembered the reality of his life.

He was blind, and there was nothing he hated more than Christmas.

Santa Claus could keep his red-nosed reindeer and stay up at the North Pole for eternity for all he cared. The truth was, Santa Claus and all the myths about Christmas were just that—myths. They were lies.

And all this maudlin musing about Christmas and his life was caused by his nosy next-door neighbor. From now on, he had every intention of keeping his distance from Tamara Knight.

She obviously believed in the magic of the season and he didn't want her to work any kind of magic on him.

Let her keep her Christmas just where it belonged. As far away from him and his house as possible.

Chapter 3

For the next few days, Kyle listened for the crunch of Tamara's footsteps on the driveway, or for her telltale knock on the door. When neither sound came, he tried to place her at the back of his mind and decided to focus on his next book. She was not coming and he felt an unexpected emptiness that left him aching inside.

He should be happy.

Kyle wanted his life to be free of complications. He should be celebrating the completion of his second book that was now sitting on his editor's desk. Instead, he was allowing a woman he barely knew to throw his life into chaos.

Christmas was drawing nearer, and the constant music on the radio and advertisements on television were almost impossible to ignore.

Add Ms. Simpson's off-key rendition of every single Christmas song ever written and he was sure to be the next patient to be admitted to the psychiatric hospital. He'd heard enough of reindeer, red noses and white Christmases to last him for the whole nauseating season.

Fortunately, his high-tech pair of headphones allowed him to enjoy the latest release from hometown-girl-turned-international-superstar Rihanna, while blocking out the noises of Christmas.

Anything to purge Tamara Knight from his consciousness!

In the midst of his thoughts of Tamara, hating Christmas and listening to music, the strangest thing happened.

The idea for his next book took root. Not in a rush of energy, but a simple, unexpected seed of creativity. He balked at the idea, but it refused to let go of his mind, springing from his imagination and forcing him into the den to record as much as he could of his initial thoughts.

He sat by the computer, the microphone from his special recording system in his hand. The story flowed for a few hours. Finally, he sat silent, exhausted by the images still churning inside his head.

He felt strange. Though writing had always come easy, he'd planned his first books in detail—chapter by chapter. This time it was different. He felt excited about his hero's next story. His protagonist needed someone to tame him, to ease the hurt of a past life steeped in tragedy.

He couldn't wait to tell Jared of the new work that needed to be transcribed. But even as he sat musing about his project, Tamara crossed his mind. He wanted to spend time with her. It was as if this creative burst from him was somehow her doing.

Kyle hesitated. Should he call her?

He'd never done anything like this before. In all the years since he'd purchased this house, he'd never visited with anyone or invited anyone over. He rarely left the house. Ms. Simpson, Jared or his lawyer usually took care of all that needed to be taken care of.

When Kyle asked Jared to take him over to Tamara's house, his assistant's only response was a soft chuckle. Kyle didn't care. He needed to see her.

A few minutes later, they stood outside Tamara's house. Kyle waited while Jared knocked on the door. He heard the click of the door handle being turned and the soft whoosh of the door opening. When Tamara spoke her voice was pleasant but cautious.

"Oh, it's you, Kyle. And you must be his roommate. How can I help you?" she asked. Her voice held a touch of formality.

What had he done? He wished the ground would open beneath him.

"I could easily say that I came to see if you had any animals that you needed help feeding, but you'd know I'd be lying. So I'll be honest. I'm bored and I came to see if I could help in any way."

"Well, actually," she said, after a short pause, "I could do with the company. I'm unpacking some boxes and you can help. Come in."

When he stepped forward, her hands took his. They were soft, and he wondered how they would feel stroking his skin.

Jared's voice broke the silence. "By the way, my name is Jared. We've met in passing before, but we were never formally introduced. I'll be back for Kyle before I leave for class, or just let Kyle call when he's ready."

"No worry, I'll bring him over. What time do you leave?" Tamara asked.

"About five-thirty. I have a class at six."

"Good, I'll bring him over before you leave. In fact, I'll even cook dinner."

"Gladys has already started dinner for tonight. I'll let her know that Kyle is having a guest. I'll see you later, Kyle. Bye, Tamara. It was a pleasure to meet you."

Kyle heard Jared's footsteps retreat. "I really don't like people talking about me when I'm right here."

"I'm sorry," she said. "I didn't mean to be rude."

"You weren't. I was just teasing."

In response, she laughed, that husky, throaty sound he could grow to love.

"Come, let's go to my office." She took his hand and he felt an unexpected jolt. He didn't move.

"Surprised you, didn't it?" she asked.

"What?" he asked.

"The chemistry. I felt it, too," she replied.

"I can see you like to speak your mind."

"Sorry, I hope it doesn't bother you. Life's a bit too short to waste time over small talk. Just promise me you won't hurt me. I don't deal with rejection well," she said with a laugh.

"I promise." He was surprised at his response. He knew he meant it.

"Good, so let's go empty some boxes."

She walked slowly, holding his hand to guide him. In his head, he started to count the way. When she stopped, he'd reached thirty steps.

"We've reached my office. Step forward and there's a chair just in front of you. You can sit there, I'll bring the boxes I want help with."

"You sure you want me to help with your unpacking? I'm not much help when it comes to things I can't see."

"But you can feel, can't you?"

"I can, so if you insist, I'll help. Just don't blame me if anything gets broken."

She did not respond. Instead he heard her dragging something toward him.

"Good, your task will be an easy one." She spent the next few minutes explaining to him what had to be done.

It didn't seem too difficult, and soon they'd developed a smooth, comfortable rhythm for moving the supplies from the boxes to the shelves.

While they worked, they chatted. Mostly they talked about her business and her dreams. Kyle was content to sit and listen.

After a short break, they continued until most of the supplies were on the shelves.

"Soon it'll be time for you to go home," she said.

"Already?" he asked. He didn't want to leave and he didn't want their time together to end. He really did enjoy her company.

"Yes, seems that time flies when you're having fun," she said.

I did have fun, he thought.

"Did you?" she asked.

"Did I what?" He pretended he didn't know what she meant.

"Have fun?"

"It was fine. It was easier than I thought. And you are a great conversationalist."

"Sorry, I can't help that. I seem to just rattle on, don't I?"

"Yes, you do. But it's growing on me."

"Oh, so I'm growing on you?"

"I didn't say that."

"Well, I'll leave you here for a short while. Since I'll be spending the evening keeping you company, I'll take a quick shower before we go over to your place. We have a few minutes before Jared has to leave."

"I'll be here. It's not as if I can go anywhere. I don't know my way back yet."

"I'll be back in ten minutes. Don't miss me too much." She laughed, her tone teasing.

"I'll try not to," he responded.

Kyle listened until he could no longer hear her footsteps.

He *was* having a good time. He felt a comfortable camaraderie with her and realized how much he missed interacting with people.

Of course, he would start thinking of her upstairs taking a shower. Again, he wondered what she looked like and knew he'd never know. But he could touch her to get a sense of her features. He'd

seen blind people do that on television often, back
when he could still see.

One memory came to his mind. A scene from
a movie he'd seen as a teenager. He'd thought the
film a bit too girly, but his girlfriend at the time
had insisted they go to the cinema to watch it,
forcing him to endure an hour and a half of un-
realistic romance.

He wanted to do that. Take his hands and place
them on her face. By touching her he would be able
to see her. He wasn't sure how it worked, but at this
moment he would give anything to touch Tamara.

He heard her footsteps before her voice interrupted his thoughts. "I'm all done. Let's go enjoy
our first date."

"Date?" he responded immediately.

"Now, don't get your boxers in a knot." She
giggled. "I'm just kidding. I would have thought
that by now you'd realize I like to tease."

"Oh, so you're a tease. I'll be sure to put that in
my diary tonight."

She laughed. "So now who's teasing? You're
definitely not the journal-keeping type."

"You've got that right. Of course, I have no doubt
that you put your secret fantasies in a little journal."

"I do, and feel no shame about it. Maybe if
you spent some time expressing your feelings you
wouldn't be so insensitive and angry at life."

Kyle stopped. "Look, if we're going to enjoy our meal, we need to try being friends."

"I thought we were friends already," she said. He sensed she was smiling.

He laughed. "Don't think we'll stop this verbal sparring, do you?"

"No, that's the fun in meeting you. I've been told I can be very intimidating, so it's refreshing to find a man who has a bit of spunk. You need to take it easy here. The steps are coming up."

She guided him down them, and they continued on their way.

"The night's beautiful, isn't it?" she asked and then paused, realizing what she'd said. "I'm sorry. I didn't…"

"It's fine," he interrupted. "Even Jared and Ms. Simpson forget at times. I don't want to have you apologizing each time it happens."

"I've never had a friend who is blind, so I'm not sure how I'm expected to act, so if I make any mistakes you need to let me know."

"Why don't you just act normal? If you make a mistake, let it be just that. A mistake."

"Sounds reasonable to me," she replied. They'd reached the patio of his house. "Well, you should know the route from here. You're on your own. We're at the steps of the patio."

"I know. I started counting from the time we

turned in the pathway. I could tell from the gravel we'd reached the entrance."

"Good, I'll follow you. It's your home."

Kyle stepped onto the patio and walked to the door, opening it. He shifted back, allowing her to enter first.

He hoped he wasn't doing something he would regret.

Opening the door had allowed her into his life and somehow he knew his life was about to change.

Tamara stepped into the foyer of Kyle's house and wondered if she was doing the right thing. His visit to her home had been a big surprise, and had served to confuse her even more.

She'd tried with all her self-control to stay away from Kyle, and had succeeded to a point. She'd actually planned to visit him tonight, but he'd beaten her to it.

Christmas was in the air and Tamara knew she was being a bad neighbor for staying away so long. She'd planned to cook up the tastiest, most succulent ribs and take them over to him.

After eating her home cooking, her stubborn, exasperating neighbor would be unable to resist her charms. She fantasized that he'd offer his hand in marriage and they'd live happily ever after.

Yeah sure, she must be losing her mind, she

thought. Kyle seemed to do that—bring out the crazy in her.

Like now, she couldn't keep her eyes off his butt. He was wearing faded blue jeans that molded to his powerful, long legs. They complemented his every fluid movement.

Kyle didn't walk, he swaggered. His strides were full of confidence and she was enjoying each and every one of his steps. She wondered if he could tell how good his rear view was.

"Nice butt," she said, before she could clamp a hand over her mouth.

When Kyle stopped abruptly and turned, she slammed right into him. Instinctively, his hands stretched out and she found herself against his body, his arms wrapped around her.

She could not breathe, her awareness of his firm, hard body heightening her senses.

And he smelled good. He had a woodsy, subtle fragrance.

"So you like my butt?" His voice was husky with emotion.

Tamara forced herself to speak. "Sorry, I didn't mean to say that out loud," she said.

"No need to be embarrassed. Feel free to look any time you want," he teased. "Just don't let me know."

She laughed, sliding out of his arms.

"Oh, I'm definitely not embarrassed. And I will look any time I want."

His returning smile tantalized her. "Good, I'm going to have to wear my jeans when I know you're dropping by."

"I won't complain," she replied. "It's good to know I have a stud muffin living next door. And Jared isn't too bad either. A bit young, but he's cute."

This time he didn't smile, only turned in the direction they were going and said, "Well, let's not stand here chatting all night. My stomach's beginning to growl, so I guess it's time I get something to eat. You hungry?"

"Definitely," she replied. "We didn't eat much today, did we? We've been working."

They'd reached the kitchen and the mouth-watering delectable scent of Ms. Simpson's cooking confirmed her hunger when her stomach grumbled again, this time louder. She could already taste the wonderful meal Ms. Simpson had put together.

"From that sound, I can see that we need to eat as soon as possible."

"Everything smells so good. I'm going to have to introduce Ms. Simpson to Gladys. I'm sure they'd love to share recipes. We can sit. The food's already set out on the table. We just have to eat."

Tamara took in the array of dishes Ms. Simpson had prepared. Two candles flickered on the table.

She waited until he moved to his usual chair, but he stood quietly by it, until she realized he was waiting for her to sit. As soon as she was seated, he followed suit, his leg brushing hers as he sat.

Heat raced up her body.

"I'll say grace," she said. She thanked God for giving them life and for the meal they were about to eat.

When she opened her eyes, he was sitting motionless, the expression on his face one of indifference.

"You're going to have to help me," he said. "Jared or Ms. Simpson is usually here."

"No problem."

She stretched across the table and took his hands in hers, pointing out where everything was. After that he seemed fairly capable of getting what he wanted from the plates.

For a while they ate in silence.

He seemed to prefer it that way. She did, too. She hated to be disturbed when she was eating.

Fifteen minutes later, they almost simultaneously placed their forks down.

"I must tell Ms. Simpson how much you enjoyed the meal."

"Was it that obvious?" she asked.

"When a woman is absolutely quiet during a meal and says nothing about where she bought her latest dress or about the latest soap opera, then she's definitely a woman who knows how to enjoy her dinner."

"I'm not sure I like your stereotyping women, but I must confess, I love a well-cooked meal. And Ms. Simpson can sure cook."

"I was lucky to find her. A friend of a friend recommended her."

"You are lucky."

"Definitely. No one wants to have to take on the responsibility of a blind man. I didn't have any family to turn to and from the time I interviewed her I knew she was perfect for the job. I was fortunate to find Jared, too."

"He's not family?"

"No. About five years ago I advertised for a live-in companion. He was the best of the candidates. He was just out of high school and looking for a job that would give him enough money to go to university. Fortunately, the government foots the bill for postgraduate education, so now he just needs the job to take care of his everyday expenses. He's now working on his master's."

"You must be close?" she asked.

"We're cool. He does what he's supposed to and I pay him well. He has a good home. He doesn't need much more." His tone remained neutral.

"So what's he studying?"

"Psychology."

"He must be intelligent then."

"Definitely. He got a full scholarship to do his master's. He asked me if he could continue to work for me and stay here. He works hard, but I'm glad to see him going out sometimes and having some fun. He doesn't do it often. Says he prefers to be at home studying."

She knew she shouldn't ask, but she did anyway. "He must like you a lot?"

Tamara watched as he breathed in deeply.

"What are you trying to do?" he finally said. "Make me into some kind of big brother? I provide enough money for someone who needs work and he works for what he earns. Don't try to make me out to be some sort of do-gooder."

"I won't. I realize you want to be this cold and indifferent Scrooge figure, but remember, even he made a change."

"Oh, I have no need for change. I'm perfectly happy with my life as it is."

"I'm sure you are. Alone in your solitary world where you don't have to face reality."

"Lady, I know reality. Reality happened to me on Christmas Eve five years ago when I woke up in hospital after the accident and couldn't see. I faced reality when I realized that all of my so-called friends were only parasites who enjoyed feeding off me. I can do without that kind of friendship."

Tamara could hear the anger in his voice. His scar seemed animated and raw.

"But I'm sure there are people who care about you. Ms. Simpson, Jared…me."

"You? You don't even know me. You've chatted with me on a few occasions and now you think you know me. Maybe you're the one who should be studying psychology," he snapped.

"Maybe I should be. Then I'd know how to deal with a pigheaded individual who seems to be happy with a sterile, unfeeling existence. Well, I'll give you your wish. I won't bother with dessert. I'll leave you to your lonely self. You seem to be the only person who makes you happy."

She stood, pushing the chair out. The loud grating noise caused him to grimace.

She hoped it pained his eardrums.

"I want to thank you for a wonderful meal. And in case I don't see you before, I want to wish you a Merry Christmas. Have a pleasant night." With that, she turned to walk away.

"Tamara." Kyle's voice was firm and commanding. She turned, wondering why he'd stopped her. "Come here."

"What is it?" she asked, stepping toward him.

When she stood in front of him, he moved forward, narrowing the distance between them.

He reached out, pulling her closer to him, and

then he lowered his head, finding her lips without difficulty.

At first his touch was demanding, evidence of his anger in the way his lips moved over hers.

And then something changed. The kiss transformed into something deeper. The anger was forgotten, leaving an overwhelming desire to taste her.

While he kissed her, his hands played a melody on her back and she found herself moving closer to him, kissing him back with a naked need that surprised her.

Several minutes later, she pushed him away, her whole body trembling with her desire for him.

Without saying goodbye, Tamara raced from the room and didn't stop until she reached the front door. For a moment she didn't know what to do.

She placed a fingertip to her lips.

She could still feel Kyle's lips on hers. She could still taste him. She needed to get away. As she opened the door and closed it behind her, she refused to look back. She knew that if she did, she'd return to the kitchen and pick up where they left off.

And then Tamara smiled.

He wanted her, she thought.

Kyle Austin wanted her.

Later that evening, Tamara stood at the kitchen sink, wondering how she was going to handle

Kyle. He continued to dig deep under her skin, and she needed to take charge of the situation. It felt strange. It was not often that she lost control of anything. Even in her early teens she'd always known what she wanted and she'd gone after it with the same fervor, drive and determination. Of course, her frequent spats with Kyle were driving her crazy since he'd proven to be a male chauvinist of the worst kind—a good-looking one.

She missed her family, especially Russell. She loved Shayne, but she could not deny the special bond with her twin. She could confirm that the psychic relationship between twins did exist. On numerous occasions during their teen years and even recently, they seemed to know exactly what was going on with each other. It was that strange connection that made them aware of each other's very heartbeat.

She moved toward the small office in the house. There was some business she needed to take care of before she retired for the night.

When the phone rang as she was exiting the house and heading to her office, she smiled.

It was Russell.

Tamara knew he'd call, but the immediacy was unexpected. Had he sensed her present state of confusion? she wondered.

She raced back into the house and headed for

the closest phone. She grabbed it before the connection was broken.

"Hi, sis. What's up? You okay?" She heard the concern in his voice.

"I'm fine, Russell."

"You sure 'bout that?"

"Nothing I can't handle. I'm a bit worried about the practice, but I'm sure everything will be fine. How's everything with you?"

"I had an interview today. Went pretty well, and I'll probably get the job. But I thought I'd call and ask you what you think. I'm not sure if I should take it. I'm really torn about staying here or coming back home permanently."

"But we talked about this. You said you'd stay in the United States for the next few years and then you'd come home."

"You know I love New York, but I love Barbados more. And I miss home. I miss you, Shayne, Gladys and all my friends."

"It'll only be for a year or two and then you'll be free to come back."

"Okay, sis, that's the reason I called. You're the one to always make me realize that what has to be done has to be done."

"And here I was all these years thinking you were the sensible one. We may both be smart, but you're the one who has the drive to be brilliant.

You'll never be happy with being a lawyer or a doctor or a vet."

"Okay, okay, let's just forget about this mutual admiration society and you tell me what's bothering you."

"Things are great, Russell. All the work on my office is complete. I'm just waiting on the supplies and office equipment, but I can't wait until the day I finally open. I'm already getting calls for potential clients."

"That's great! But remember, life is not only about working oneself to sleep each night. It's much more."

"It is?" she teased.

"Yes, it is."

"And this coming from the man who studied more than I did. I may have gone on to veterinary school, but you're the one with two undergraduate degrees."

"Well, it's not my fault I'm smarter than you."

"Yeah, that's true. You were the one with all the A grades."

"You didn't do too badly yourself, sis."

"So where is the job?"

"It's an internship at *The Times.*"

"*The Times?* You mean, *The T-I-M-E-S?* My brother's going to be working at *The Times?* Is the money good?"

"Definitely. It's more than good. I have my professor to thank. A friend of his called and asked for an intern. A new program they're working on. He recommended me."

"Have you told Shayne? He'll be so excited."

"I'm giving him a call as soon as I've finished talking to you. How're plans going for your opening?"

"Fine. Of course, Shayne has been dropping by to help."

"I don't doubt it. Big brother knows best."

"He *has* been a lot of help. He's only ever wanted what was best for us."

"He has always supported us in helping us succeed and work toward our dreams."

Russell paused for a moment. "So are you ready to tell me what's bothering you?"

Tamara realized there was no sense in hiding what was going on. "Do you remember Kyle Austin?"

"I'm not sure, but the name sounds familiar."

"He was a cricketer. He went to school with Shayne."

"Yes, I know who you mean now. He was in a serious accident a few years ago, wasn't he? I always wondered what happened to him."

"Well, I know where he is."

"Where?"

"He lives next door to me."

"He does? I remember when he used to come to our house."

"Russell…he's blind."

"Blind?"

"Yeah, he lost his sight in the accident. That's why he disappeared."

"You've met him?"

"Yeah, I've been over to his home a couple times. I'm worried about him."

"Tamara, I hope you don't feel that he's one of those 'patients' you've been bringing home since you were a kid. He's not a hurt animal. He's a man."

"I know, Russell, but he needs to get out of the house. He doesn't go anywhere. Would you believe he wants nothing to do with Christmas?"

"Now, that's really bad. Wow, I'm so sorry to hear it. No Christmas gifts for him."

"Russell, I can do without your sarcasm."

"Okay, you're your own woman. Just let me give you a warning. Remember that time you brought home that cat you found? Remember how it turned on you and almost scratched your eyes out?"

"But that wasn't the cat's fault," she protested. "If you hadn't scared her, she would never have acted like that."

"See, you're always making excuses for those animals of yours. Just do what you think is best and make sure you don't get hurt."

"I won't, Russell. I know what I'm doing."

"Oh, well. You and your strays."

"He isn't a stray. He's a human being who needs help and I have every intention of helping him."

"You wouldn't be the kindhearted person you are if you left him alone. Sis, I really must go or I'm going to have to send you my phone bill. Love you."

"Love you, too," she said, and then she heard the line click as her twin disconnected the call.

When she put the phone down, she wondered about what Russell had said. Looking back, she realized she did have a history of bringing home strays. It was all part of who she was. She couldn't bear to see an animal hurt and defenseless. She would be the first to admit that she'd always had a soft spot for animals.

She remembered a day long ago when she was nine. She'd accumulated so many stray animals that her father had finally discovered her secret. She'd hid all of her little creatures in the large dollhouse.

Yeah, she did have a soft spot for animals, but Kyle was totally different.

He was not an animal.

He was very much a man.

Chapter 4

Kyle couldn't help it. Tamara made him so angry, but he couldn't help being stimulated by the feisty, outspoken woman. There was something about her that just made him feel more alive.

He ached. He didn't know what had possessed him to kiss her, but at that moment, he'd just wanted to. He smiled, remembering the kiss. It'd been like one of those soap opera moments when the man reaches out and kisses the woman thoroughly and then she slaps him in his face and they kiss again.

There'd been no slap and no second kiss, but he'd enjoyed the one. He savored the soft taste of a woman. It'd been too long since he'd had a woman in his arms. He realized how much he missed that feeling.

Tamara had smelled good. There had been no overpowering fragrance, just the subtle hint of flowers about her. He'd wanted to bury his face in her neck and inhale her sweet scent all night.

He'd felt totally disappointed when she pulled away and he'd forced himself not to draw her to him again.

He knew that he was crazy to think of ever getting involved with Tamara Knight. The woman was trouble and he couldn't afford to let anyone or anything disturb his calm, comfortable existence.

She was making him think of other things; things he dared not wish for. He was happy with Jared and Ms. Simpson and if they left him, he'd simply find someone to take their places. He had the money, so replacing them wouldn't be a problem. That night in bed, he tossed and turned. Sleep was way out of his reach. When he'd had enough, he rose from the bed, feeling his way to the window and pushing it open. A cool blast of air struck him in his face and he shivered.

He inhaled deeply, as if hoping to catch a whiff of her on the night air. But all he smelled was the sugary scent of the ripening cane fields. It reminded him that harvest time was near.

It was hard to remember the last time he'd cut a piece of the juicy ripe stalk and sucked its sweet nectar.

There were so many aspects of his life he'd taken for granted before the accident. There were so many places on the island he'd promised to visit. Growing up, he'd always heard of the wonder of Harrison's Cave, but he'd never visited there. Now he would never see the place islanders considered one of the wonders of the modern world.

He heard a car pull into the driveway. That would be Jared.

He felt for the hands of his watch. It was 11:30.

Why couldn't that boy enjoy himself more? He remembered the nights when he'd be out until the crack of dawn. When Jared did go out, he was always home before midnight. He heard the car stop and waited for the telltale sound of the door opening.

Minutes later, Kyle heard footsteps come up the stairs and along the corridor before stopping outside his bedroom. There was a sharp knock on the door.

"Come in," Kyle said.

He heard the click of the door and then Jared's voice.

"You're still up. Can't sleep again?"

"Not really. I was just thinking about my next book." He didn't want to admit it, but he found it difficult to sleep whenever Jared was out late. At least there was something good about the fact that the boy didn't do it often.

"You had a good time?" he asked.

"It was okay. Lots of my friends were there so it wasn't too bad."

"Hope you don't plan to study all night. You need to get some sleep."

"No, I'm going right to bed. I can stay a bit if you want me to. Until you get sleepy."

He was about to tell Jared there was no need when he changed his mind.

"Yeah, that's cool. I could do with the company."

There was silence. He knew Jared was surprised at his response. It was not the first time Jared had offered to stay and chat. But this was the first time Kyle had accepted Jared's offer. Kyle had always told him there was no need.

In that moment, Kyle realized something. He knew nothing at all about his employee's life beyond the past four years. He didn't even know if he had a family.

Kyle did know when Jared's birthday was, but that was only because Ms. Simpson never failed to celebrate it. He also knew Jared's age. Those were basic facts. But Kyle knew nothing about

Jared's life before he'd come to work for him. And now, for some strange reason, a part of him wanted to know all about the boy.

Maybe he'd been stupid to keep their relationship on the level he had.

"So how's the studying going?" He felt awkward, but he knew that he needed to do this.

"It's going fine. Just one more semester and I'll be done. I've done all my course work, and I only need to submit the first draft of my dissertation to my supervisor, but she's pleased with my proposal and what I've done so far. I have until the end of August next year to make my final submission," Jared said.

"Which means you won't be able to enjoy Crop Over?"

"It doesn't matter. I'm happy just to listen to the new calypsos on the radio."

For a moment there was silence.

"Kyle, can I ask you a question? I don't want you to think I'm being presumptuous, but is there a reason why you don't like Christmas?"

That was not the question Kyle had expected and he wasn't sure if he wanted to answer.

"You don't have to answer if you don't want to." Jared always seemed able to read his mind.

"I had my accident on Christmas Eve. I don't know if I'm being silly or not, but the season holds no good memories for me."

"I'm sorry. I wish you didn't feel that way. My memories of Christmas aren't all good, but at the home they always made it special for us."

Kyle didn't know what to say. Jared had been raised in a group home?

So they did have some stuff in common!

"You grew up in a group home?"

"Yes, when my mother was sent to prison, I was placed in the system. I stayed there until I was eighteen. By then I'd decided I wanted to go to university. I wouldn't have been able to do so without this job." He paused. "And you."

"You worked hard at school?"

"Yes, I saw it as the only way for me to get out."

"I had no idea," Kyle said.

"You haven't wanted to know before. And I'm not one for saying much either, so since you seemed happy to consider me just an employee I accepted that. I'm accustomed to being on my own. Remember, I grew up in foster care and the word is always *survive*. It was never good to attach yourself to anyone, since you never knew when they'd be gone, too."

"Doesn't sound like it was an easy life."

"Not really. But all of that's behind me now. I'm doing well. Thanks to you, I have a good home."

"We've not been too close, have we?"

"Not really, but I understand," Jared said.

"Because you think I see you as an employee."

"A bit, but I've learned to accept it."

Kyle didn't know what to say. Somehow he felt as if he should apologize.

"I'm sorry."

"No need for it. I know what it's like. You've had to deal with a lot more than I've had to deal with," Jared said. "But you don't have a lot to worry about these days. You have a beautiful vet falling for you," Jared teased.

"She just feels sorry for me." Kyle knew he was beginning to sound pathetic.

"Okay, if that's what you think. But I'm watching to see how this romance develops."

Kyle snorted. "Romance, my ass."

All Jared did was laugh.

"You want a beer or something? I'm not too much in the mood for studying tonight. The exam today was pretty tough, but I still did well. Hey, I know—how about we go downstairs, you warm up that leftover pasta, and we listen to some music?" Jared suggested.

"Sounds good to me. But I'm sure my music may be a bit too old for you."

"See how much you know about me. What music do you think I listened to for the past four years?"

"I'll wait and see. You go warm that pasta and we'll chill for a while. You have a class in the morning?"

"No, classes are over. I only have to go to the library later in the day. I'll have the stuff warmed up by the time you get downstairs. You just get the music kicking."

Jared closed the door behind him, entering his room and glancing around. He never ceased to be amazed at his fortune. Who would have thought that the poor black kid who'd grown up in foster care would turn out to be a university scholar?

He placed his laptop on the desk he used to study and stripped off his clothes. Damn, he was tired. His thesis was consuming a lot of his time, but he was feeling pleased with his research.

This weekend he intended to take a well-deserved break from studying. He'd go to the beach tomorrow morning and take in a movie in the afternoon, after he left the library.

He didn't go out much, but this weekend would be the exception. With his high grade point average he could afford to take a break. His academic achievement had helped him to make something of himself. He had no intention whatsoever of returning to where he'd grown up. As soon as he'd finished high school he'd looked for a job during the summer and had made enough money to buy his books. Thankfully, the government paid the full cost for tuition.

His thoughts strayed to the man he now worked for. In his early teens he'd worshiped the man. He didn't know why fate had smiled on him, but he'd been fortunate. He'd seen the advertisement for a live-in companion to a blind man and he'd jumped at the opportunity. He got the job.

Now, four years later, he still didn't know why Kyle had chosen him. He was no companion. Just an assistant who worked for money he thought was way too much for what he did. In the early stages of his job, he'd tried to do more, tried to reach out to his hero, but Kyle had maintained a distance that often left Jared feeling sad.

Somehow, in his naive imagination, he'd seen them becoming friends, like brothers. He didn't need a father, but a big brother would have been nice. Not that they didn't get along well, but he hated the formality between them.

He wished that he could talk to Kyle, but Kyle was as tortured a soul as he was.

But he was noticing the slightest change in his employer, and Jared suspected the pretty doctor from next door was responsible for it. In the years he'd taken care of Kyle, he'd never seen him so flustered. Kyle seemed to exist because he had to.

The only thing that had taken him in a positive direction toward recovery was his writing.

Despite his limitation, Kyle had learned to tap into the world of his imagination. Jared loved the stories his boss created. The first book in the series had captured his attention and he felt privileged to be in a position to read it before it came to print.

In fact, when he'd found Kyle dictating the story one day he'd stopped and listened, entranced by its power. He'd told Kyle how he felt about the story and the fact that it was good enough for submission. He'd even offered to modify his duties to do the transcription. Of course, his grumpy boss had not thanked him personally for volunteering. But the first month after assuming his new duties, Jared had seen a significant increase in his paycheck.

But in his young mind, he'd wanted more from his boss. He wanted to share his dreams with Kyle and ask for advice about girls. But nothing had changed between them, just his salary.

There were times when he'd wanted to reach out to Kyle, but somehow Kyle would always erect a wall between them. A wall that Jared was unable to climb.

He remembered clearly his first Christmas with Kyle. He'd spent more than four weeks searching for the perfect gift for him, hoping that it would somehow bridge the gap between them. Instead, just before Christmas, he'd been told bluntly that Christmas wasn't celebrated in the house.

Jared had been disappointed. Despite his past home life, Christmas had been a time of celebration, even in the group home. He would wake up on Christmas morning and race to the old, fake tree that the home put out each year. There had always been something waiting for him under the tree.

That was Christmas. The rest of the year would be days and nights of quarreling between the other boys. He'd stayed away from the home as much as possible, only going there to sleep. He'd spend hours in the library until it closed. That was the reason he'd done so well at school. The library had been his sanctuary.

But he'd ached for some form of affection. He'd just broken up with a girl he'd been seeing on campus.

Oh well, that was life. But somehow he knew things were about to change. He'd just spent a few hours with his boss, with Kyle, and it had felt strange. They'd taken a step forward and they might finally be friends, he thought.

Yeah, things were changing.

He had no doubt that Tamara Knight had played a part in this transformation.

And one thing he was sure of…she loved Christmas.

* * *

So he'd been a jackass, but two days without hearing her voice was more than he could handle right now. When Jared returned he'd ask to be taken next door. He suddenly realized something: he needed to be more independent. For years he'd flinched at the thought, but he'd finally concluded that all his money couldn't buy what he really needed—his independence.

He looked back at the past few years and realized he'd done nothing whatsoever to deal with his blindness. Instead, he'd paid money to get people to become his eyes, hands and feet.

He was pathetic. He was going to do things differently from now on. Of course, there were things he couldn't do. But he needed to get around the house and its close environs. He still had no intention of going out in public though. And he still wanted to avoid the press.

He really didn't want anyone dropping by for an interview to find out what he was doing with his life. That much he wanted to keep private. But maybe he would take Tamara up on her invitation to visit Shayne. He remembered Shayne and his two best friends, Troy and George. He'd wanted so much to be a part of their small group and they'd indicated that it was cool with them. But when he'd discovered his skill at cricket he'd had no

time for friends who didn't share his interest.
Shayne, Troy and George had been brains, and
they preferred to spend most of their time at their
studies. Not him. He'd been all about the game.

Tamara had enough of being stubborn. She was
going to swallow her pride and go next door. Kyle
Austin was constantly on her mind and she had to
do something about it. There was no sense in pre-
tending that she didn't want to see him again.

She'd been in the garden when Jared left and
he'd waved at her. They spoke briefly before he
told her he was on his way to the cinema.

"You can go visit Kyle if you want to," he'd told
her with a smile hovering on his lips.

When she'd failed to respond, he'd said with a
measure of maturity in his voice, "I don't want to
seem presumptuous, but Kyle needs some company, and you're the first person I've seen who can
make him come alive. But it seems you're just as
stubborn as he is."

She watched as he walked away, knowing that
what he said was true.

So here she was, putting the finishing touches
on dinner before she went over for a neighborly
visit. Of course, she'd made enough for Jared, too.

Half an hour later, dressed in a pair of faded
jeans and an old T-shirt, she headed next door.

When she reached the end of her short driveway, she stopped briefly. She could see Kyle.

He sat on the verandah.

His head turned in her direction and he smiled. He'd heard her footsteps.

"Didn't think you'd drop by after our last meeting."

"Oh, I don't stay angry for long, but it did take me a while to forgive you."

"Forgive me?"

"Yes, I've only been trying to be a friend, but with each act of kindness you never fail to be rude."

"Unfortunately, I can't help it. I have a grouchy disposition."

"I'm quite aware of that. Of course, I'm not particularly fond of your Scrooge-like behavior."

"Scrooge?"

"Yes, Scrooge. You haven't read Dickens' *A Christmas Carol?*"

"I wasn't much for reading when I was at school, but I have heard of *A Christmas Carol.*"

"Then you really should read the book. I'll be sure to get you a copy for Christmas."

"I'm not much for Christmas."

His voice had gone hard, cold. She realized that she had to change the direction of the conversation, or dinner would be over before it started.

"Well, I've brought dinner for you…and me. Of

course, there will be enough for Jared, too. You hungry?"

Tamara saw the brief hesitation, but his face remained unmoved.

"Yes, I'm hungry," he replied. "Whatever it is you've put together smells divine."

"Good. I spent quite a while getting everything just right. And I'm starving."

At her words, Kyle rose from the chair. "Come, let's go in. It's getting chilly out here."

She followed him as he opened the door and moved down the hallway.

As she walked behind him, once again she could not help but look at his backside in the shorts he wore. The shorts clung to him, and were evidence of the fact that he must work out. His well-toned thighs and calves bunched as he walked.

He turned into the kitchen. He felt briefly for a chair and sat, before saying, "Help yourself. Plates and cups are in the cupboard directly in front of me. The knives and forks are in one of the drawers below. And of course you can see the microwave if you need to do any reheating. I'll take care of the drinks, if you let me know what you want. I have lemonade and iced tea."

"Oh, the lemonade would be fine."

As she moved toward the cupboard, she watched as Kyle skillfully took care of his part of the meal.

He removed a pitcher from the refrigerator and then took two glasses from the cupboard. He rested the glasses on the table, then poured the lemonade into them. He didn't spill a drop.

"There was no need to stand and watch me," he said. "I'm quite capable of getting simple things done."

Tamara felt the heat in her face and knew that she was being silly.

"I'm sorry. I didn't mean to be rude. It's not often I get to see a blind person at work."

"Oh, there's a lot of things that I can do. Especially if I'm inside the house. Outside, I'm hopeless."

"You could get someone to work with you, to help you to be more independent. It would make things a lot easier for Jared and Ms. Simpson," she said. Tamara moved quickly to pull their meal together, taking the fare from the small basket she carried. She hoped she hadn't put her mouth in where it didn't belong.

"Oh, I'm quite happy as I am. The farthest I have to go is the patio. Ms. Simpson and Jared usually take care of everything else. They get paid to do it."

Tamara placed plates brimming with layers of potato and chicken on the table. She made sure she placed his fork in its familiar position. She'd leave it at that. She had no intention of arguing with Kyle.

"Well, we can eat," she said.

"Thanks," he said. "It smells delicious."

For a while they ate in silence until she remembered the trend of their conversation.

"So how long has Jared been working with you, again?"

"About four years now. Just before he entered university I hired him. He's done his three years of undergraduate work and is in the final year of his master's program."

"You must be pretty proud of him."

"Tamara, as I've said before, don't go reading into the relationship I have with Jared. He's just an employee. It's been like that from the beginning and I'm happy with things exactly as they are." Before the words slipped from his lips he knew he was lying. He wasn't sure what was happening to him, but he didn't like it one bit.

He did know that the hint of her perfume was assaulting his sense of smell. Everything about her did this to him. He didn't want this. He just wanted to enjoy the dinner and the company of a beautiful woman. He could not see her, but Jared's description suggested that she was stunning. And even if Jared hadn't described her to him, deep in his heart Kyle knew Tamara was lovely.

"Are you planning to finish eating? It's the first time I've prepared dinner for a friend and he spends the whole time talking instead of eating," she commented.

"I'm sorry. It tastes divine, but something important was on my mind."

"I was about to think I'd lost my touch."

"No," he said, filling his fork and lifting the food to his mouth. "It's amazing."

The spicy tang of curry and chicken tickled his taste buds.

For a while he was silent, savoring the delight that was each morsel.

When he'd cleaned the plate completely, he turned to her.

"Your description was an understatement," he said. "You are a great cook. Let me know who taught you and I'll marry her today."

"I'll pass on your proposal to Gladys. I'm sure she'll be delighted. Unfortunately, she doesn't cook too often anymore."

"I remember Gladys. She's your housekeeper."

"*Was* our housekeeper. We forced her to retire last year when she turned seventy-five. Now she's a lady of leisure. Of course, she still cooks occasionally, but we thought it was time she retired. She went out screaming, but she'll be the first to admit she's enjoying her retirement. I'll bring her over to meet you when she comes to visit me. I'm sure she'll be glad to see you," Tamara said.

"I met her years ago when I visited the plantation and your parents were still alive," Kyle replied.

He stopped. Silly him. He'd brought up her parents' deaths.

"It's no problem. I hardly remember them. They are just fond memories. It was all because of Gladys and Shayne that Russell and I were able to adjust to life without our parents."

"Well, you do seem to have adjusted well. What made you want to become a vet?"

"I'm convinced I was born to be a vet. From the time I was a child I always took care of hurt animals. Until Shayne decided that the best thing to do was let me work at a vet's office during the summer. And I also love horses. Of course, you know that since I have my two beauties in the stables. You must let me teach you how to ride."

"In case you've forgotten, I'm blind."

"And what does that have to do with anything? Blind people can ride."

"I'm sure they can, but I have no interest in learning."

"Why is it that you're happy to go through life with this attitude? It seems like you're scared to do everything."

There was silence.

"I didn't mean to say that. It was mean of me. I have no idea what it's like to be blind."

"No, you don't, but you're always trying to tell me how to live my life." She could hear his voice straining with anger. She'd gone too far.

"I'm sorry. Maybe I just think you can do much more than you're doing. You seem happy to sit at home doing nothing. I'd be bored."

"I don't sit at home all day doing nothing. You'd be pleased to know that I'm actually employed."

"So what do you do?"

He hesitated, unsure of whether he should let her know, but his need to win her approval somehow forced his secret out.

"I write."

"Write what?" He heard the humor in her voice.

"Have you ever heard of K.C. Austin?"

"Yes, it's that Barbadian author who made it big in the U.S.," she replied. "No. That's you?"

"Yeah, I'm K.C. Austin."

"Wow! So that's what you've been hiding out here doing? I'm going to have to get a copy of your book. I was planning to buy it just to support a local author, but each time I go into the bookstore, I end up buying the latest romance novel. But I know I've seen a copy of your book at the plantation house. Shayne's wife Carla must be the one who bought it. I don't know the last time I've seen my brother read a book that doesn't deal with agriculture or the economy.

"So you're K.C. Austin. I'm living next door to a true celebrity."

"And I'd prefer if you'd keep it our little secret."

She did not respond. Kyle began to feel apprehensive.

"What are you thinking about?" he asked.

"I was thinking I'd like to kiss you," she replied.

He felt his heart stop. He wasn't sure what to say, but he knew he wanted to kiss her, too.

He felt her breath on his face, knew she was close.

When her lips touched his, he felt his body tremble. Her touch was light, a caress, but he wanted more and knew she was giving him the chance to take the lead.

She tasted like the strawberry cheesecake they'd had for dessert. Her scent was different. Instead of the freshness of before, he noticed the distinct fragrance of a long-forgotten fragrance his mother used to wear.

He felt for her, easing his body against hers, drawing her closer. Her body felt good against his and only served to arouse him more.

She felt good, more than good. He reveled in the feel of having a woman in his arms again.

At that moment, he realized something. He was going to claim Tamara as his.

As he kissed her, his hands roamed, wanting to

touch her all over. He ached to caress her breasts. He knew they'd be small and firm.

She moaned, he groaned, and then she pushed him away gently.

"I think we'd better slow things down a bit," Tamara said, her breathing deep and heavy.

"I agree. We don't want to do something either of us is not ready for. However, I can't promise you I won't want to kiss you again," he said.

"It's going to happen again, Kyle. You can count on that."

And with those final words, he changed the conversation, but the promise lingered in the air.

Chapter 5

Tamara pulled the covers tighter around her. She was freezing cold and wide awake, but the air-conditioning had nothing to do with it.

She slipped from her bed, moving to adjust the thermostat. When she was done she moved toward the window and pushed it open.

Her glance moved toward the direction of *his* house and she noticed a shadow moving outside.

Was it Kyle?

Jared?

She reached for a T-shirt and a pair of sweatpants and slipped into them. She'd take a short run and maybe she'd be tired enough to fall asleep when she returned.

She headed downstairs and walked out into the night. Keys in her pocket, she jogged down the driveway. She glanced in the direction of Kyle's house again. Someone was sitting on the patio.

When she reached the road, the person stood and jogged down the driveway, heading in her direction.

She slowed down, knowing it was Jared. Tamara welcomed the company.

When he reached her, she stopped.

"Hi," he said. "Seems we had the same idea. Mind if I join you?"

"I don't mind the company. You think you're up to it?" she asked.

"Oh, I'm sure I'm up to it. I've been doing this for quite a while. I didn't get the chance this morning since I was up so late last night. Wasn't planning on it tonight, but I couldn't sleep."

"Same thing here. Sleep seems to have eluded me recently," Tamara said.

"I must thank you for dinner. It was great. You must be one of the best cooks I know."

"Thanks. I'm glad you enjoyed it. However, if we continue to stand here chatting we won't get much jogging done," she observed.

"How long do you run for?" Jared asked.

"Half an hour most of the time. Forty-five minutes if I want to push it."

"Good, I'll work up a good sweat." He moved off and she quickly joined him.

The night was a beautiful one. The full moon above provided a path for them to travel easily. The only sound that could be heard was the staccato pounding of their feet on the asphalt road.

Beside her, Jared kept pace, slowing when she slowed and quickening his run when she increased her speed.

Half an hour later they returned home, their breathing hard, but controlled.

When they stopped back at Kyle's driveway, Jared turned to her. "You want to sit on the patio for a while? Want a bottle of water? Lemonade?"

For the briefest of moments, she hesitated, and then said, "Sure, some water would be nice."

"Good. I wouldn't mind the company until I'm feeling sleepy. I'm sure I'll sleep well tonight."

Jared turned and headed up the driveway. Tamara followed.

When they reached the patio, he said, "Sit here. I'll be back in a minute."

After Jared opened the door and stepped into the house, Tamara lowered herself into one of the patio chairs and closed her eyes. The night was silent with just the faintest breeze.

She opened her eyes when Jared returned. He handed her a chilled bottle of water. He eased himself into the chair next to hers with a heavy sigh.

"You tired from the run?" she teased.

"A bit, but school has been really stressful lately with the research I have to do. I'm working on my thesis and it's taking up most of my time. Fortunately, we're on holiday now so I can get a bit of a break."

"You'll be able to enjoy Christmas?"

"Not really. We don't do much Christmas stuff here. Kyle's not into joyous cheer."

"He isn't? Why not?"

"I'm not sure, but he had his accident the day before Christmas."

"He told you…about the accident?" Tamara asked.

"No. Kyle doesn't talk much about himself. In that way, he's a lot like me."

"In what way?"

"We both grew up in a children's home."

"Kyle was raised in a group home?"

"Yeah, but I'm not sure why he ended up there," Jared said.

"I didn't know that," she said.

"I don't think there is much people know about him and he has made sure it's kept that way."

"Is that the reason he doesn't like Christmas? Because it brings back bad childhood memories? Does he have any friends?"

"Not that I know of. I've never seen anyone visit. Just his lawyer. Actually, he never leaves the house much."

"Well, we're going to have to do something about this situation."

"We?"

"Yes, we. You care about him. I can see that you do."

"I just work for him," Jared said.

"Yes, you work for him, but it's more than that."

Jared sat quietly for a moment. "Okay, I care about him. He's like the brother I never had. I know him better than I know anyone, but I still don't really *know* him."

"You're hurt because he's so distant, aren't you?"

"Maybe a bit," Jared admitted softly. "I just wish I had someone to talk to about my problems. Someone to turn to when I want advice. I've tried to bridge that distance between us, but the divide just keeps getting wider and wider."

"Sometimes things take time," Tamara said.

"Oh, I don't let it worry me anymore. I'm too old for that. I realize that I just have to take care of myself. At least I learned that a long time ago in the home. It's all about survival."

* * *

Kyle moved away from the door, hoping that the spots on the floor that had a habit of creaking would not break the silence.

He'd moved from the den when he heard the voices. He'd heard Jared's at first.

When he'd realized the second voice was Tamara's, the unexpected rush of jealousy had stopped him in his tracks.

Didn't she know she was too old for Jared? But in reality, he knew they were only a few years apart.

Maybe it was for the best. Perhaps if she were to start dating Jared he would forget about her. And truth be told, he and Tamara could never get together. A relationship with her would be too complicated.

When Kyle heard her laughter, he knew it was time he moved away from the door.

Walking as quietly as he could, he moved toward the den. He wanted to write some more, but he would never be able to concentrate on his work, particularly at this time of night.

Music would be the only thing that could calm his current state of mind.

He entered the den, moving toward the chair where he usually sat when he needed to relax. Sitting, he reached for the headphones and put them on. He heard the spin of the five-CD changer and sighed in contentment as John Legend's raspy tenor filled his head. The artist didn't have the greatest voice, but few singers could infuse the emotion he did into a single line.

Kyle loved his voice. A voice that was warm and reminded him of love, lovemaking and the promise of happily ever after. His eyes closed as the music seeped inside and touched the very core of his being.

And for the moment, he could leave the world with its crazy roller coaster of emotions behind him.

When the music stopped an hour later, Kyle rose, headed to his room, got into bed and fell asleep.

He dreamed of Tamara Knight. The soulful voice of John Legend provided the soundtrack as he made love to her again and again...

In the morning Kyle woke before sunrise, just after five. The bits of conversation he'd heard the night before floated in his mind. His emotions ranged from anger to sadness. He hadn't listened to the entire conversation, but he knew he hadn't liked what he'd heard.

Tamara actually thought he was weak and needed to let go. She actually still believed that he'd not come to grips with his blindness. But he had done all he could in the past years to come to grips with his blindness.

Or had he?

He could take care of himself. He showered and dressed himself. He could move around the house without any help. So what if he had the money to hire someone to help take care of him? It was his right. And damn her if she felt it was a sign of weakness. He didn't much care what she thought.

He was proud of who he was—blindness and all. He knew where he'd come from. In the early part of his career, he'd done everything possible to keep his past hidden and he'd succeeded. That was one of the reasons he loved living in Barbados. The paparazzi and gossip magazines were almost non-existent here. There were no nosy journalists trying to pry into his past—a past he wanted desperately to forget.

Often in the middle of the night, during his recovery from the accident, he'd find himself transported to a time when he'd been happy. But that time had been long before the accident, when Christmas and love were still a part of his life.

He didn't want to take himself back there. He didn't want to face returning to that part of his past, but somehow he found himself drifting back to a time when he was happy, before his parents died and he found himself tossed around in the foster-care system.. He heard his mother's voice, loud and clear as if it were yesterday…

* * *

"Kyle, you comin' to get the bowl? It's all yours."

He raced into the kitchen, coming to an abrupt stop when his mother scowled at him. He knew what was coming. It was a standard battle between them, but it was all part of the love between them.

"Kyle, what I told you 'bout running in the house?"

"I'm sorry, Mom."

"Okay, you go wash your hands. You and those boys spend all your life playing cricket. You hungry?"

"Yeah, I'm starved, but can I lick the bowl first?"

"So why do you think I called you?" she said and laughed.

Kyle rushed to the bathroom to wash his hands and returned to the kitchen in record time.

His mom was singing a song about a white Christmas and he joined her despite the fact that the song lost its meaning in the hot sunshine of an island where snow never fell.

Later that night, he sat with her around the Christmas tree, his heart beating fast. He just gave her his gift, a bottle of perfume he'd purchased with money he'd been saving for months. He knew his would be coming next.

When she left for her bedroom and returned a

few minutes later, he almost screamed with joy. He knew exactly what his gift was.

When he opened the box and found the bat he had asked Santa for, he felt unexpected tears in his eyes.

He looked up at her, his smile wide and excited.

"Thank you, Mom. You're the best mom in the world."

The memories of a time that had been special in his life made him pause. He'd loved Christmas back then, but so much had happened in his life since that time. Now, he didn't feel that Christmas was all it was made out to be. He realized that Santa Claus didn't exist. Now he knew that stores used Christmas as a time to swindle thousands of dollars out of the pockets of unsuspecting shoppers who felt they needed to shop to keep the holiday spirit alive.

He still remembered his mother, that strong hardworking woman who'd made every Christmas special. Until one Christmas he'd raced home from the pasture nearby where he and the boys still played cricket.

He'd found her lying on the floor in the kitchen, a bowl of dough on the floor beside her. She had to be admitted to the hospital that day.

That year, he'd spent Christmas all alone. That year, he'd stopped believing in Christmas and

Santa Claus. Christmas, which had always been so important to his mother, no longer meant anything to Kyle. How could God have allowed his mother to get ill on Christmas of all days?

From then on, Christmas had been like any other miserable day.

And then the accident five years ago had only confirmed his feelings about the holiday. Christmas was a day that held only bad memories for him.

But some things in his life were changing. He was remembering how much his mother had loved Christmas. His relationship with Jared seemed to be expanding. And his emotional response to Tamara suggested that his attitude toward women might also be undergoing some changes.

He'd not had any physical contact with a woman in years. At first, he'd been frustrated by the need to release himself. He needed to feel a warm supple body under his, but the feelings had faded until he pleasured himself on those rare occasions when his long-buried sex drive reared its head. At those times, he could only take matters into his own hands.

But even then he felt no satisfaction, only a dull emptiness. He'd shrugged his shoulders and moved on with life.

No, Tamara only served to cause his appetite for sex to awaken from a long sleep.

She tantalized him, and even though he couldn't see her, he ached for her touch.

He wanted her. He needed her so badly he felt as if he were going crazy.

What worried him most was that his craving wasn't all about making love to her. He wanted to *be* with her. Somehow she stimulated his mind, making him think with every challenge she threw his way.

And that need for her scared him.

Tamara heard the scraping at the door. Someone or something was out there. She stood slowly, moving toward the door. Turning the light on, she peered through the frosted glass windows and saw a small dog standing there, his gaze focused on the door.

He was looking up as if waiting for someone to come. Her heart melted when she saw him, but she knew better than to handle a dog without the proper equipment.

Heading to her office, she grabbed her bag and headed back to the door.

The dog was still standing there when she returned. She slipped on a pair of gloves and then opened the door.

He stepped back, his eyes wary. But she spoke gently to him. He sat there and refused to move closer.

"Come on," she said. "No need to be afraid. I'll take care of you."

But the dog refused to move. He just sat there and looked at Tamara, who eventually lowered herself to the steps and sat by him.

It was always a matter of time and patience, she thought.

After fifteen minutes the dog stepped forward and sniffed her cautiously.

Apparently satisfied that Tamara wouldn't hurt him, the dog sprawled out next to her and promptly rested his head in Tamara's lap. After a moment, he closed his eyes and slept.

Tamara sat still and waited until the dog awoke. He shook his head and stepped toward the door of his new home.

"No, no, no. You don't belong in the house yet. I'll take you to the examining room and run a few tests and make sure you're fine."

When she took the dog in her arms, he didn't protest.

Twenty minutes later, washed, dried and sore from his shots, the dog lay quietly in the stall she'd cleaned out for him.

He would sleep for the rest of the night, but she'd come and check on him in the morning.

She moved back to the house. She'd call Kyle

before she went to bed. Jared had given her the telephone number and she needed to talk to Kyle.

Jared picked up on the phone's second ring.

"Hello, Austin residence."

"Jared, this is Tamara. I'd like to talk to Kyle."

"Can you hold on? He's upstairs in his room."

She heard him shout for Kyle and then she heard the click of an extension.

"Hello. Kyle speaking."

"This is Tamara."

"And how can I help you, Dr. Knight?"

"To be honest, I have no real reason for calling. I just wanted to hear your voice."

He did not respond immediately.

"I'm glad you called," he said eventually. "I wanted to hear from you, too."

Now she was at a loss for words. She hadn't expected this response.

"I don't like what's happening to me," she said.

"What *is* happening to you?" he asked.

"I'm thinking about you—a lot."

There was silence. She couldn't breathe. She dreaded what he would say.

When he finally spoke, his words surprised her. "I've been thinking a lot about you, too. And I'm not sure I like it much either, but I can't, won't, fight it anymore. I've lost total control of my thoughts."

"You have? You always seem so in control."

"I thought I was…until I met you. I've had to deal with a lot in the past few years. But I finally felt content with my life until a pushy, beautiful woman came along and disrupted everything. To say I wasn't ready for the chemistry between us is a huge understatement."

"So you think I'm beautiful?" she teased, her voice subtly coy.

"I got the information from a secondhand source, but I consider him quite reliable. Maybe you should describe yourself to me."

"Describe myself?"

"Yes, tell me what you look like," he prompted.

"This is silly," she said.

"I'm serious. If you would tell me what you look like, please."

"Okay, but only because you said please. I'm tall—just under six feet. My hair is brown and reaches below my shoulders. My eyes are brown, pretty ordinary. Some people say I have a stubborn chin."

"Do you wear dresses?"

"Oh, I prefer jeans and T-shirts. I've always been more of a tomboy."

"You don't have a tomboy's voice. You sound all woman to me. But you say you prefer jeans and a T-shirt?"

"It's just that I liked playing sports in school

and swimming. I've always preferred casual clothes. However, I still like to dress up on occasions, so I'm definitely still in touch with my feminine side. Maybe one of these nights you can take me out to dinner so we can dress up."

"Maybe," he replied unexpectedly.

"No argument? I expected a totally different response."

"No argument. I'd decided it makes no sense arguing with you. You're determined to make changes in my life and routine. We'll see how it goes." He paused for a moment. "And now, I'm beginning to get tired and need to get my rest, so I'm going to say goodbye."

"I'm feeling a bit tired, too. I'm going to read a bit before I go to sleep. And don't forget you're going over to Shayne's with me on Sunday. I've invited Jared, too."

"Thanks. It's good for him to get out sometimes."

"Well, have a good night."

"You, too. Sleep tight and don't let the bed bugs bite."

"So you're trying to say that my bed has bugs?"

"Tamara, I know you want to stay and talk to me all night, but I really must be going."

All he could do was laugh when he heard the phone slam in his ear, but not before he heard her say, "Insufferable ass."

When he crept between the covers several minutes later, he was still smiling.

Insufferable ass, indeed.

She wanted to call him more than an ass. Did he really feel that she wanted to continue talking to him longer?

Heat spread across her face.

He wasn't far from the truth. She'd enjoyed chatting with him. She liked the witty verbal sparring. Their words had been heated with innuendo and promise.

She wanted him and her desire scared her.

He'd continued to work his magic on her and work himself under her skin. She could feel his presence constantly.

She could tell that he was battling her intrusion into his life. She wondered if she was doing the right thing. He seemed content with his life, but she couldn't help it. She couldn't stand the thought of him spending the rest of his life locked away from the outside world. Not that she wanted him back in the limelight, but she knew he needed to get back into the world of the living. He could not continue to exist in the sheltered world he'd created. He was a vibrant, lively man who'd allowed his blindness to reduce him to a pale image of his former self.

He was a challenge, but he was much more than that. She wanted to help him to live again.

Tamara knew beyond a doubt that she was having an effect on him. She was attracted to him and knew that the feelings were mutual.

His being blind didn't worry her. She was sure they could have a normal relationship. He couldn't see. That was all. As far as she knew, all of his other organs were functioning properly.

Of course, all indications were that he'd not had sex in years. Fortunately, Tamara didn't mind in the least giving Kyle a helping hand back into the saddle, so to speak.

Her thoughts appalled her, but she didn't care. She wanted him and she knew in her heart that they would be lovers. She had every intention of making sure it happened.

She was probably thinking like a hussy, but if seduction was necessary she'd put on her best red dress. Actually, the color of the dress didn't matter much, did it? He'd never be able to tell what color she was wearing, but she'd make sure to wear a dress of the softest fabric so that when she trailed her hand along his arm, he'd feel every wisp of the silk against his skin.

Oh, well, she couldn't spend all night thinking about Kyle, Tamara thought. She had lots of things to do tomorrow. With Christmas just a short week away she had to make sure that everything else was done in a day or two.

She wanted to spend time decorating the house and that would mean going into the city to buy what she needed. Of course, on Friday she'd have to go back home to help Carla and Gladys with the plantation's decorations.

She wanted to be there. She wanted to see her nephew, too. Darius was growing like a weed.

And then the unexpected happened. An image flashed in her mind of her body swollen with Kyle's child.

She wanted children. She wanted one of each—a boy and a girl. One looking just like her and the other, hopefully, the spitting image of Kyle Austin.

Yes, maybe she was going too far with her fantasy. She hoped her obsession with him would not be considered stalking, but she had nothing in common with the groupie type that she knew had harassed him in his days as a star athlete.

She stood, moving away from the television that she hadn't been watching and headed upstairs.

Time for a shower, bed and then dreamland. For each night now, dreams of Kyle Austin lulled her to sleep.

She had no doubt that tonight would be no different.

* * *

The next day, Kyle found himself in a mood he didn't particularly care for. In fact, he'd been cranky and irritated for the past few days. Tamara was really working her female mojo on him. She'd made him feel emotions he thought had been buried forever. At times, he'd been angry. At other times he'd felt totally alive. Today, however, he felt...nothing.

Moreover, he didn't want to *do* anything. He just wanted to stay in bed and pull the covers over his head.

It was the first time in months he'd felt this way. After the accident, he'd awakened feeling like this—absolutely depressed—often, but he'd slowly managed to work his way out of it. He was just musing a way to snap out of his doldrums when he heard a knock at the door.

Despite telling Jared that there was no need for the morning pleasantries, the boy still insisted on looking in on him before he left each day.

"Kyle, I'm on my way out. I'll be in the library as usual. Need me to pick up anything for you on my way home?"

"No, I don't need anything," he replied abruptly.

"I've left breakfast on the stove. You only need to put it in the microwave to warm it up. Ms. Simpson says she'll be in a bit late. She had to go to the supermarket to pick up a few groceries."

"Okay, okay, you can go now."

There was silence.

"You okay, Kyle?"

"Damn it. I'm okay. Why don't you just go?"

There was silence again, and then the slow retreat of footsteps.

What was wrong with Jared? In the past they'd gotten along fine and now all of a sudden he was trying to change things.

He didn't want it. For a moment, when they had talked earlier that week, he'd melted. But he realized there was no sense in making more of the relationship than what they'd already established. The boss-employee thing had worked well for almost five years, so why spoil it with complicated emotions now?

But somehow he knew they could not go back. Their talk the other night had changed their relationship. Jared was no longer just an employee. He was a person with a past and a future…and someone Kyle cared about.

He hadn't wanted to admit it, but one of the reasons he'd hired Jared was that the boy had seemed so much like him.

Not the studious part of Jared's personality. On that trait they were as different as night and day. But Jared had ambition and Kyle had known that there was something in the boy's past that mirrored his own background. Jared had seemed like a lost soul. And in that he was like Kyle, too. However much he tried to convince himself Jared was only an employee, deep down inside he'd always wanted to make sure the boy had a chance to succeed in life.

He sighed.

His life was becoming so complicated.

He felt so tired. He was tired of fighting, tired of feeling crazy and tired of feeling lost.

And he hated being blind. After five years he still hadn't come to terms with his condition.

Yes, he'd learned to deal with some aspects of his handicap, but he didn't think he'd ever truly accept it.

He rose from the bed, stumbling as he stepped to the ground. He was allowing his current mood to make him careless. He seldom made mistakes. He made sure that everything was always in its place.

He walked toward the window. He felt like screaming. Maybe he should scream. The only person who'd hear him would be the one who he blamed for everything that was happening to him.

He inhaled deeply. He could tell the difference between this part of the island and the more urban areas.

He couldn't see, but his heightened sense of

smell made him aware of the subtle changes in his environment. He loved the breeze that smelled fresh and felt soft and light against his cheeks.

He pushed the window open a little more, feeling the light chill of the morning air. He took another deep breath and then turned toward the bathroom.

Maybe things wouldn't be all that bad today. His mood shifted with the soft wind that now blew through the room. Perhaps he needed to make some changes. Change could sometimes be a good thing, he thought. And sometimes change was necessary. He was a different person. He hoped a better person. But then he wondered what he would have turned out to be if he'd not become blind.

Of course, he'd have been one of the greatest cricketers ever. He'd be married and probably have one or two mistresses.

He didn't even want to think of that. But the lifestyle he'd been living before his accident had pointed in that direction. Maybe the accident had saved him from himself.

He missed playing cricket and he knew he'd never play again. But maybe he could do something else. He didn't know what, but the current state of West Indies cricket worried him. He'd try to think of something. He'd try to think of some way he could make a meaningful contribution to the sport.

So what were his plans for today? He hadn't planned on doing any writing, but he thought he should. He needed to write. Then he'd go next door. He'd call Tamara and ask her if he could come over.

He knew she was probably annoyed with him. He was sure he was sending mixed signals, but that was exactly how he was feeling. He was all mixed up inside. It wasn't something he had much control over.

He moved toward the bathroom, took a shower in record time and headed down the stairs.

After a good breakfast, he moved to his office.

He'd spend a few hours recording his next book since he had not done much over the past few days. His young hero had much to say.

Another confession he had to make. His hero was a lot like him, or, at least, a lot like who he wished he'd been as a teenager. Instead of a noble individual, he'd been caught up in the big-ego thing. Being the best of a young crop of cricketers hadn't helped.

Young Nkosi, his African hero, was a boy who saved the world. A boy who lacked all the negative characteristics he'd possessed at that age.

Maybe it was time he became that hero.

But heroes were only part of a fantasy world people created to try to make the world a better place. That was all in books and not the reality of the world he lived in—a world that had taken his vision and transformed him into a shell of the man he'd once been.

But here he was demeaning himself again. He'd done some things in the past few years. His agent had told him that his book was being read by both boys and girls all over the world. He'd found an audience, one he hoped would continue to increase with each new title.

Okay, but no more musings. He needed to spend the next few hours writing....

"Kyle, please come to the principal's office."

He stood, wondering what was wrong. He hadn't done anything. The last time he'd been in trouble was when he, Shayne, George and Troy had skipped class to avoid a test. It'd been a stupid thing to do. They'd been sent to detention for a whole week, but it had taught them a valuable lesson. They'd been good for a few months after that little incident.

He walked slowly to the principal's office with a feeling of dread.

When he reached the office, he hesitated at the door. "Kyle, the principal is waiting. You can go right in," the secretary had said.

He stepped forward and entered, surprised to see the school's counselor in the principal's office. Something was definitely wrong.

"Kyle, sorry to take you from class, but I have some bad news for you. I'm sorry, but your mother has passed away."

He wasn't sure if he'd heard right, but the two faces before him spoke the truth.

He wasn't sure what was expected of him. Was he supposed to cry? He didn't want to at this moment. He just wanted to run from the room. Instead, he just stood there, not focusing on anything.

The counselor came to him and placed her arms around his shoulders. "Come, we'll go to my office. A relative is coming to pick you up."

His uncle. His mother's brother. He was the only family Kyle had left.

An hour later he sat in his uncle's car, his eyes focused on the passing cane fields that somehow seemed to be waving at him.

"You can come live with us, but you're going to have to share a room with your cousin Sean."

"Thank you," he found himself saying. He knew that his uncle was being kind, but he wondered how his aunt would take all of this. Ever since his uncle got married, he'd kept his distance from Kyle and his mother. His aunt came from a wealthy

family; she'd always acted as if Kyle and his mother were beneath her.

"I'm sorry I haven't come to visit, but you know how things are."

"Yeah, I know how things are. Are you sure your wife will be okay with me staying with you?"

"She'll be fine, Kyle. You're my nephew. I won't let her come between you and me. Right now, you need to think about your mother and the good times you had together."

"Why did she have to die, Uncle Paul? Why did she?"

His uncle pulled over to the shoulder of the road and stopped the car. He took Kyle in his arms.

The tears came now. Kyle allowed them to pour down his cheeks as he grieved for his mother. Somehow, he knew that things were going to change, but for now, he couldn't be strong.

It was ten days after Christmas, but on the radio, Nat King Cole was still singing about chestnuts and open fires, and for the first time, Kyle hated it....

He'd not remembered that incident in years, but the memory was as vivid and clear as if it had happened yesterday.

His mother's illness and death had been his first traumatic Christmas. Unfortunately, he'd had many sad holidays since then, including the most devastating holiday five years ago.

But today he didn't want to think of sad memories. He wanted to think about happier things. He wanted to hear from Tamara.

He reached for the phone but quickly put it back down.

He picked up the phone again and dialed the number now logged in his mind.

His heart, always so normal, beat faster as he waited to hear her voice.

Chapter 6

Tamara heard the phone ring, but her hands
were filled with boxes of supplies that she needed
to unpack.

If the call were important the caller would leave
a message, so she ignored it and continued toward
the office.

There she emptied the final boxes of stationery
and her office was complete. She was ready for
her grand opening in two weeks' time and there
was nothing else to be done except wait for the
telephone company to install the new phone
system.

She slipped behind the desk and sat in the large

black office chair Shayne had given her. She knew he was proud of her, and his gift had made her cry. She was grateful for his confidence in her and his pride in her achievements. Of course, she'd also been embarrassed because she was not one for crying.

Now she needed to check on the animals. She especially wanted to see to the dog that had appeared at her door. She needed to see how he had fared during the night.

When she pushed open the door to the kennels, the dog immediately stood, his eyes filled with the same wariness she'd seen in them last night, but his tail wagged.

Tamara held open the kennel door and waited for the dog to step out. Eventually, he cautiously came forward.

Bending down, Tamara ruffled his back, and he looked up at her with sad, lonely eyes.

It seemed she had another dog to take care of, she thought. And then she had the most wonderful idea, though she decided to run it by Jared before she acted on it.

It was the perfect solution. She'd give the dog to Kyle as soon as she was sure it was safe to be around people. He'd been pretty comfortable with her, but Tamara didn't want to take any chances. Of course, she had to do the right thing and put an announcement in the newspaper to see if the dog was lost. If no one came forward to claim him, the little guy was going to Kyle.

In the meantime, she'd invite Kyle over and let him become acquainted with the little thing. She was sure he'd love the dog.

She picked the pup up, holding him gently as she looked him over. Before she returned to the main house she made sure he'd eaten. She also took him for a short walk outdoors. Back in the kennel area she let him follow her around.

She hoped she didn't fall in love with this pup before she turned him over to Kyle.

When she returned to the house, the pup close behind her, she remembered she needed to check to see if the caller from earlier had left a message. There was none, but the caller display indicated that either Kyle or Jared had called.

She picked the cordless phone up and dialed the number.

Kyle answered on the first ring.

"Trying to avoid me?" he asked.

"Yes, but I decided you'd be too upset if I didn't call back."

"Touché," he said, laughter in his voice. "I deserve that."

"You do." Her laughter echoed his. "So what can I do for you, Mr. Austin?"

"I just called to find out if you'd have mercy on me. I'm bored."

"Bored? I'm surprised. I was so under the impression that you were happy with your life. I'm not sure how I can assist you in relieving your boredom."

"I could come over and help you do some stuff around the office."

"Sorry, all my office stuff is done, but you could come over to help me feed the animals."

"Of course I'll help. I'll come over right now. I'm already dressed."

"Is Jared there?"

"No, he's gone to the university."

"Want me to come get you?"

He hesitated. The number of steps to her house came to mind. He'd counted them the last time he'd visited. "No, I'll get there. Just wait for me by the patio."

"Will do," she replied, before she heard the click of the phone disconnecting.

She restrained herself from rushing to the front door. He had to do this on his own. When she glanced out the window several minutes later, he was already making his way up the driveway.

Though he walked slowly, there was confidence in his step and when he reached the stairs to her patio, he stopped.

"You plan to stand there all day or are you going to help me?"

She was glad he couldn't see the tears in her eyes. She didn't want to say anything since she was choked up, and she knew he'd hear the emotion in her voice. She stepped forward and took his hands.

"So you did make it on your own. I'm proud of you," she eventually said.

"You didn't think I would." He sounded disappointed. But to be honest, she should have known he would have made it.

"Yes, I knew you would."

"Don't say that just because you think I want you to say it."

"I'm not. I knew you'd make it. I didn't expect you to make it so quickly."

"Smart response," he said.

"I may think you're hiding out here from the outside world, but I've seen your stubborn determination. You'd have gotten here even if it took you a whole hour."

He smiled as if her answer pleased him. "So where are we off to, Ms. Knight?"

"Oh, we're going to feed the few animals I have here and then we're going to take a walk in the pasture just behind our houses. There's a wonderful spring that runs there." And to make sure she'd convinced him to go, she asked, "You sure you're up to it?"

"Of course I'm up to it," he said, irritated that she might suggest he wasn't.

Good, her strategy worked. She knew he wouldn't be able to refuse the challenge.

She took his cane and rested it on the chair on the patio. Then she reached for his hand and they walked silently to her office and then the kennel area.

When they arrived in the place where the animals were, the dog jumped up, immediately wagging his tail. He stopped when he noticed that Tamara was not alone.

"No need to be afraid, boy. He's a friend." At her words, as if the dog understood, his tail began to wag furiously again. Tamara let him out of the kennel, and he rushed out, barking and jumping in excitement.

All Kyle did was stand silently.

"You want to feed him for me, Kyle?"

"Just tell me what to do."

"I'll make this easy. I'll give you a tour around the main office and the other rooms and let you get a sense of them. Then I'll let you feed him."

Fifteen minutes later, armed with a large bag of dog food and a bowl, Kyle sat and filled the bowl with the two cups of chow and moistened it with a half cup of water as Tamara had instructed.

When Kyle placed the bowl on the ground, he heard a yelp of appreciation and the sound of crunching as the dog devoured the meal. The dog's presence brought back a rush of memories.

His uncle had given him a dog one Christmas. Unfortunately, that had been the final straw for his uncle's wife, Stella.

He'd seen the guilt in his uncle's eyes when he'd driven him to the place.

"Uncle," he'd said, "I know this ain't your fault. Don't worry about me. I'll be okay." With that, Kyle had taken the bag that contained all that he had and walked away without looking back.

At that point he hadn't cared about whether he'd be adopted or not.

Kyle had been glad to leave his uncle's house. He could no longer bear the tension and hostility from his aunt. From the beginning she'd done everything in her power to force him out. In the end, his uncle had been forced to make a choice between his wife and his orphan nephew. He'd chosen his wife.

One thing he could say was that his uncle had made sure he was provided for.

In the first home in which he'd been placed, his foster mother had been horrible. The old lady had been a mean hag. She'd worked him to the bone all the while, calling him every derogatory name she knew.

But he'd endured her cruelty. He'd eventually discovered that the woman was Stella's aunt. Ironically, in the time he'd lived there he never saw Stella drop by.

Fortunately, he'd been able to play cricket after his chores were done and he'd entered one of the leading high schools on the island. Yes, he'd done the minimum of work, but by the time he was eighteen and school was over he'd been offered a place on the West Indian team. One of the youngest players to be offered a contract.

When the old lady passed away, he'd been surprised she'd left the house to him. He'd sold it without a morsel of regret.

The coldness of something wet drew him from his memories. It was the dog. Its tongue against his hand tickled.

The pup had placed his head in Kyle's lap.

Instinctively, he reached for the dog, holding him gently and placing him in his lap.

"He likes you," Tamara observed.

He didn't respond. When the dog curled himself in his lap and rested his head against his stomach, Kyle experienced a strange feeling. Nostalgia. The image of his first dog became clear in his mind's eye.

"What kind of dog is he?" he asked.

"He's a German shepherd mix. About six

months old. Someone left him outside my office last night."

"What are you going to do with him?"

"I have a couple choices."

He kept listening.

"Have you ever thought about getting a guide dog?"

His immediate response was to shout no. Didn't this woman ever stop pushing? And then the dog licked his hand again.

"To be honest, I've never thought about it, but I'm not sure what to say."

"He's at the age when he could start training in a few months and in five to six months he'd be your eyes. He'd make you a lot more mobile. And he likes you."

As if to confirm what Tamara had said, the dog whined and licked his hand again.

"I'll think about it," he said, his tone not totally convincing. "I promise."

"Okay, that's all I can ask for now. I'll go over and feed the horses. You stay and keep him company. Maybe give him a name before I get back and then we'll go on our picnic."

While she was gone, Kyle sat, talking quietly to the dog.

The little fellow so reminded Kyle of his first dog. Kyle thought about naming the dog something silly like Spud, but because the dog was destined to be his, he wanted to name him something he could live with. A name like Spud would get old really quickly, he thought. He needed to name him something more dignified.

It was curious, but thinking about a name for the dog made him think about his uncle. He'd only seen his uncle a couple times over the past few years. He'd always sent the older man tickets for his matches, but they rarely visited one another. After the accident, he'd heard that his uncle had immigrated to Trinidad, where he'd been offered a job. That was the last he'd heard of the man.

Kyle sighed. So much for family and so much for his old life, he thought.

He turned his mind away from the past and back to the present. At this moment, he was looking forward to going on this picnic with Tamara. He hoped that somewhere between the fresh air, the hike and lunch that he'd get the opportunity to kiss her again. It seemed that during the past few days, kissing Tamara and the past were all he could think about.

When Tamara returned, she found Kyle talking to the dog. The dog was looking up at him with absolute adoration and Kyle's face carried a similar expression.

Things had gone better than she'd expected. They were bonding. Of course, she was sure they wouldn't want to be separated by the time the day was over. If the dog was good guide-dog material, she would make sure he went into formal training. They would make a great pair, she thought.

"You ready to go? I'll just go back to the house briefly and get our picnic lunch together."

"Can the dog come with us?"

"Sure. No name yet?"

"Yeah, we decided on Alex."

"Alex? That doesn't sound like a dog's name?"

"It isn't, but a dog can have any name," he said.

"How about a dog name like Bruno, Rex, or Rover? Those are all good dog names."

"I don't want my dog to have a doggie name."

Tamara smiled. He didn't realize what he'd said. "Okay, Alex it is. Are you ready for that picnic?"

An hour later, they sat on a blanket under the shade of an old mahogany tree that grew in the large pasture behind their houses. Someday, she planned to build a corral for her horses in this area. She wanted to wait a year or so before she made any additions to her not-yet-opened practice. She could see young boys and girls riding around the corral.

The day was a beautiful one. After eating several barbecued chicken wings, macaroni pie and potato salad, Tamara was totally full.

Kyle burped politely, said, "Excuse me," and thanked her for a wonderful meal. Then he stretched out on the blanket and fell asleep. Alex lay next to him, fast asleep, too.

While he slept, she used the opportunity to take a good look at him.

His body was hard, and his lean frame and height made him very imposing. His hair was short, cropped close almost to his skull.

She tried to take her eyes off the generous bulge in his jeans, but it wasn't easy. He was handsome in a pretty kind of way, but there was nothing feminine about Kyle Austin.

He had perfectly trimmed sideburns and a goatee. His dark complexion glowed with health, so she knew he took good care of himself.

The overall picture was of a man who was too handsome for his own good, but one who no longer used his attributes to control those around him.

Tamara believed there was a reason in life for everything. Perhaps Kyle's accident and resulting injury, and her moving next door, were changes dictated by fate.

She noticed that his lips moved slightly. When she leaned close to him, she heard an incoherent whisper.

And then she really noticed his lips for the first time. They were slightly full and aching to be kissed.

As she watched him, he awoke, rising slowly

up. Alex raised his head as if realizing his new master was awake.

"You had a good hour of sleep."

"Damn, I feel good. I needed that. I haven't been sleeping well lately."

"Have things on your mind?"

"No, just a person. A beautiful Bajan girl." She heard the teasing in his voice and decided to play along. "Want to hear who she is? You need to come closer," he said.

Tamara obliged, moving closer to him. Despite the bright sunny day, lightning flashed and Tamara could not help but groan.

She placed her lips next to his ear and said, "So you going to tell me who this incredible woman is?"

"Oh, I don't want to waste time talking, demonstrations are a lot more effective," he replied, his voice husky with desire.

With that he reached for her, holding her firmly before pulling her into his arms. He gently caressed her lips with his.

In the distance she heard Alex barking. He must be chasing something, she thought. But she put the dog from her mind and concentrated on the kiss.

No, not a kiss.

What they were doing was much, much more. Before she knew it, Kyle had removed her shirt.

His hands moved to her breasts, his touch making her nipples painful and turgid.

She didn't realize what had happened until she felt the fuzzy texture of the blanket against her back. She was lying down and Kyle's body was pressing against hers. He was heavy, but her only thought was of how warm her body felt. She felt a telltale tingle between her legs where the full, pulsing length of Kyle's penis pressed against her.

She wanted him.

When she felt his mouth against her breast, she smiled, loving the gentle caress.

She loved the feel of his chest against hers.

When had he taken his shirt off? She didn't know. Didn't care. She just wanted him close to her, on top of her.

When he rolled onto his back, still holding her tight, she followed and wantonly straddled his body.

She glanced down at his erect penis, and she reveled in the control she had over him.

She wanted to give him equal pleasure. When she placed her lips on one of his eager nipples, his husky moan only served to excite her more.

He'd taken his sunglasses off and for the first time Tamara saw the color of Kyle's eyes up close. Tamara gasped as she looked into his usually cold, black eyes. Their dark, unseeing depths glowed with passion.

Tamara shifted her hand between them, touching his hardness and felt an unexpected jerk. Again, Kyle groaned.

And then the unexpected happened. He groaned even louder and shuddered with an intensity that left him breathing deeply. She placed her arms around him and held him tightly.

When the spasm stopped, she continued to hold him, loving the feel of him. She hoped he wasn't embarrassed.

When he spoke, there was laughter in his voice.

"I really didn't expect that to happen. Damn, I'm going to have to call myself Quick Draw McGraw. I guess the years of inactivity have made me a bit too sensitive."

"I wouldn't worry about that. I promise we'll be doing it again, so practice will make perfect."

"How can you be so flippant at a time like this?"

"Because life is too short to worry about things that I have no control over. And for the record, I'll be very annoyed if this happens again," she said playfully.

"Oh, we'll be fine next time," he said. Then added, "And there will there will be a next time."

"Of course," Tamara said. "There will definitely be a next time."

While she spoke, she caressed him tenderly. She was glad he hadn't been embarrassed. He'd laughed it off and made her a promise that left her anticipating their inevitable joining.

"That's good to know. I'll look forward to it," he said.

"Good. Want to take a stroll with me before we leave? There's a great spot just up ahead."

As had become the norm, she took his hand and led him toward the line of mahogany trees.

Letting him sit on a large boulder first, she made sure he was comfortable before she sat.

For a while they sat there, enjoying the tranquility of the surroundings. She enjoyed the panoramic view stretched out before her.

"Can you describe what it looks like to me? What do you see?" he asked.

"I'm sorry. I'm looking across the St. Thomas Valley toward Bridgetown. In the distance I can see the ABC highway and since it's early evening already, the highway is flowing with traffic. Just to the left there's the harbor and two large cruise ships are docked there."

"Damn, I miss being able to see. Ironically, if I weren't blind, I probably wouldn't take note of or appreciate any of what you're describing. One of the things I've learned is that too often we're surrounded by beauty and never get the chance to really see it."

"What you say is true, but that's true for people

who can see, too. We spend so much time rushing around that we don't get enough time to appreciate our other senses," she said.

They were silent for moment.

"Have you ever really sat down and listened to the sounds around you?" he asked.

"Not really," she replied. "I just hear ordinary things."

"So let's do it. Let's spend the next few minutes just listening," he suggested.

Tamara closed her eyes and listened. At first there was nothing, just the honking of car horns in the distance, but then she began to notice other sounds.

She heard the rustling of the wind in the branches of the trees above and then the screech of a blackbird.

She heard the flapping of wings. But she not only experienced the sounds around her, she was now also aware of the scent of freshness in the air.

Her body still tingled with the memories of Kyle's touch as well.

She opened her eyes. Kyle's face carried a picture of absolute rapture, like a child who has just discovered something strange and wonderful.

"So how was it?" he asked.

"You were right. It's beautiful to just sit and listen," she said.

She wanted to ask him a question, but she hesitated. She didn't want to spoil the mood, but she asked anyway.

"Did you lose your sight in the accident, Kyle?"

She saw the torture on his face, and then he seemed to gain control of his emotions.

"I was in a coma for three weeks. When I woke up, something felt wrong. It felt as if I had a heavy weight on my eyes. I put my hands up to push it away and realized nothing was there. I panicked because everything was dark. The next time I woke up I was a lot more lucid, but realized what was wrong.

"So many tiny particles of glass had flown into my eyes that most of the nerves were damaged and I couldn't see. The ophthalmologist said there was nothing he could do."

"No operations were possible?"

"None. And that made me very angry. I cursed the world and everyone in it for months before I faced reality. I was blind, period. The night of the accident, I'd just taken my fiancée out to dinner and was taking her back to my home to give her a necklace I'd bought her for Christmas."

"Is that why you hate Christmas so much?"

"A bit of it. Christmas holds too many sad memories for me. My accident, my mother's death. I remember all those things at Christmas," he said.

"But maybe you need to create new, happy memories. I'm sure you had some good Christmases before your mother died. Wouldn't celebrating Christmas honor her memory?"

"I've never thought of it that way, but we'll see. You never know. By the time the season is over, I may just be aching for it to come again," he said quietly.

"We'll see," she replied.

It was then she felt the first drop of rain. She looked up at the sky. A few dark clouds to the east seemed to be coming in their direction. The wind rustled the leaves in the trees that stood, limbs outstretched, waiting in anticipation for the moisture.

"Come on, Kyle Let's get back to the house. The rain is coming," Tamara said, raising her voice to be heard over the storm winds. She grabbed his arm and they quickly walked back to the picnic spot where she packed everything back into the basket.

A few minutes later, the slight drizzle turned heavier and she hurried Kyle into her house.

"You're going to have to stay here until the storm blows over. You can get out of those wet clothes and take a shower if you'd like. I have a pair of jeans and a shirt that Shayne left here. I've washed them and you look like you're about the same size. You can wear them," she said.

"I'm sure the rain will be over in a few minutes," he said.

"Sorry, I won't take no for an answer. You'll take your shower and then I'll take mine and we'll watch one of my favorite movies. Later, I'll take you home. Do you think Jared will be back yet?"

"I don't think so. This morning he told me he wouldn't be home until after nine tonight," Kyle said.

"Good, it's only a bit after five now. We have all evening to have fun. I'll show you to the shower and I'll start dinner. I'll come back up when I think you're done," she said.

Upstairs, she showed him how to work the shower and the path he'd need to take to reach the bedroom. She put his hands on Shayne's clothes, which she'd laid out on the bed. She rested a chair close to the bed and left him to get into the shower. She headed down to the kitchen. She'd come back in half an hour and he should be done.

When she pushed the bedroom door open to leave, she looked back and immediately stopped in her tracks. She had forgotten to close the bathroom door.

Kyle had slipped off his shirt and was about to take his jeans off. Her breath caught in her throat.

His shoulders were broad and he had a neat, trim waist for a man. It was his buns that really caught her attention. Firm, smooth and rounded. She wanted to rush back into the bathroom and join him, but it wasn't the right time. She wished it would be soon, but it wouldn't be right, not now.

With a willpower she didn't know she had, she turned away from the wonderful sight. She closed the door quietly behind her, hoping he didn't realize the tantalizing view he'd just given her.

Outside the bedroom, she leaned against the door. *Damn*, that man was fine!

Chapter 7

Kyle heard a slight sound when he rested the pants in the basket Tamara had pointed out to him.

She'd left a few minutes ago, but he was sure it had been the door that just clicked shut.

So she was trying to get a look at his naked body. Tamara wouldn't do that. Maybe she hadn't shut the door properly and it just closed itself with the gentle breeze.

Oh, well, it didn't matter whether she'd seen him naked or not. In time she'd see all of him. And feel him, too. He had every intention of making love to her.

Kyle stepped into the shower cautiously, unfamiliar with the layout. Once inside, he ran his hand down the wall in front of him, feeling for the faucet. Adjusting the water to a comfortable coolness, he savored the sense of control he was feeling.

Not that it was going to help for too long. As long as he stayed close to Tamara, his nerves and every fiber in his body were on high alert.

And then it happened. That slow building of awareness as his penis took on a mind of its own as he thought about her.

A bolt of intense pleasure shocked him. He wanted Tamara and he didn't think he could wait any longer.

He knew he wanted her. Perhaps, if he let her know all the things he wanted to do to her, she might agree to let him do them.

He slipped from the shower, put his hand out to push the bathroom door open and realized it was open already. So she'd seen him undressing. He hoped she liked what she saw. If he had his way she was going to see a lot more of him.

He sat on the bed and waited until she returned.

Almost as if she'd heard him, the door opened and he heard her brief gasp of surprise.

"I thought you'd be dressed by now. I'm sorry," Tamara said.

"No problem. I wanted to make sure you got a good look this time," he said.

"A good look? Is something wrong?" Her voice drew nearer.

"Yes," he replied, but said no more.

He felt her presence before him. He could hear her steady breathing.

He stood, feeling her body touch his. He felt his body stirring.

He reached for her, placing his arms around her and drawing her closer.

He was getting good at this.

She smelled good. She smelled like the scent of rainwater and the freshness of the flowers.

"You want to get in the shower with me?"

She did not respond for a while, but when she did, her answer came heated with emotion, a hint of laughter in her voice.

"I didn't realize Christmas was coming early this year. Give me a minute," she continued, "while I get out of these clothes."

A few seconds later, Kyle felt her hand take his and he followed her. He felt her hand around his waist, and the towel fell to the ground. For the briefest of moments he felt embarrassed. Tamara was the first woman to see him naked in years, but the old music sang to him, and the rhythm began to flow.

Reaching for her, he pulled her into his arms

again. The need to kiss her was so overwhelming he couldn't wait.

"I could kiss you right now, but if I do I won't be able to stop," he said.

"Then don't stop. We can take that shower later when we need to. Now, I just want you to make love to me," she said.

Her lips covered his as she took control. And he joined her, kissing her back, tasting her very essence, tongues entwined, and he heard her groan of pleasure.

"It may be better if we go to the bed," Tamara said.

He smiled his agreement.

"Your wish is my command," he said. "Since I'm blind I'm going to need all the help you can offer."

"Oh, I'm sure you'll do fine, Mr. Austin."

She led him to the bed. When he felt her hands on his chest, he sat down, the momentum taking her with him.

They were a tangle of arms and legs before Kyle felt her softness against him. He wished he could see her.

And then he smiled again.

He could see her…with his hands.

"Can I touch you?" he asked.

"You are touching me already," she replied. He heard the laughter in her voice.

"I mean, really touch you. I want to see you," he whispered.

"You can do whatever you like," she said. Her voice was husky with desire.

He flipped her over gently, his hand immediately searching for her face.

"Close your eyes. I don't want to hurt you," he said.

He felt her nose, the delicate curve of her neck and her slender shoulders before he cupped each of her breasts, enjoying their firmness.

Kyle moved lower, touching the tight muscles of her stomach and then the delectable curve of her hips.

His hands brushed over her and, without thinking, he lowered his head, placing his mouth on the gentle mound.

Using his fingers he gave himself access, easing his tongue inside her and pleasuring her.

He inhaled her scent, a healthy scent with just a hint of exotic flowers.

Beneath him she wriggled and moaned, her face revealing the strength of her desire. He felt her hands on his head and raised it.

"I don't have any protection," he said.

"It's okay. I do. I made sure I bought some a few days ago."

"You were pretty sure of yourself, weren't you?"

"Not really, but I was optimistic," she said.

"Then I'm going to have to give you your wish."

"Give me a minute," she said.

Her body slipped from beneath him, and he lay on his back, feeling exposed. His erection was hard and throbbing, and he ached for relief.

He felt a coolness on his penis and shuddered as her hand worked the condom down its length.

He sucked his breath in, trying not to lose control.

When she was done, he felt her body shift from above him and move to lie next to him. He turned his body, balancing himself on his elbow above her.

He felt her lips touch his and they kissed again. Their wet, hungry kisses grew more fierce, a raw indication of the intense desire they felt for one another.

Her hand touched his sheathed penis and he knew she was guiding him toward her. When he entered her, her muscles contracted, but he still felt her slippery readiness.

And then he started to move, slowly at first, allowing her to get accustomed to his length and thickness.

Tamara groaned, and her legs widened to take him deeper. He could wait no longer. He thrust into her completely, his gasp of pure delight echoing hers.

He eased himself out and back in again. Tamara's legs wrapped themselves around his back, drawing him even deeper inside, until he completely lost control.

There was no time for gentleness. He could sense that her need matched his own, so he increased his pace, entering her time and time again, with long, strong strokes that made him want to scream.

Instead, he whispered in her ears. Erotic things that made her more excited. They were partners in a wicked, witty exchange of sound and sweet nothings.

And then Kyle felt it, the tensing of his muscles and contraction of his penis and he knew he was near climax.

Her body reacted and he could feel her need for release, too.

"Come with me," he whispered as the music of a lone steel drum played in his mind.

And as the sound of the pan intensified, Kyle thrust into her one final time before everything around him exploded. For the briefest of moments, he saw her in his mind's eye as she, too, screamed her release as spasm after spasm took control of her body. He sighed as she, too, gave in to that sweet helplessness that leaves lovers breathless.

For a while they lay in silence.

"You want to take that shower now?"

"I'd love to, but my legs are so weak I don't think I can move," she said.

"It's only your imagination. I'll help you," he said.

"Can't I just lie down and sleep?"

"Nope, we're going to take that shower if I have to drag you in there," he said.

Five minutes later, with water cascading down their bodies, Kyle entered her again. This time, he slowed the pace, savoring every moment of making love to the most beautiful, passionate woman in the world.

With Tamara's back against the wall, he entered her slowly and deeply, each stroke a movement of precision as he touched each of the sensitive points of her womanhood.

And in no time, his cries of joy joined hers and his legs grew weak and he almost fell with the intensity of the release.

In the back of his mind he heard a voice cry, "I love you," but he knew it wasn't his voice. He was definitely not ready to make that kind of commitment yet.

That night, when Jared entered the house, he was surprised to find it empty. Where was Kyle? he wondered.

What a silly question. He was willing to bet

that Kyle was over at their beautiful next-door neighbor's house.

He wondered if Kyle had gotten himself some long overdue loving. Man, things must be better than he thought between those two.

He glanced over at the Knight house and noticed the lights were off.

It was late. He'd call and ask Kyle if he was coming home. That would be a discreet way to find out what was going on. He hoped that was where Kyle was. Tamara was the perfect person for Kyle. She was just what Kyle needed.

In just two short weeks of knowing Tamara, Kyle had moved from being a grouchy hermit into a man who was on the brink of a life change. Sure Kyle was scared of the change he was going through, but in the end Jared was convinced that Tamara would be good for Kyle.

All was for the better. He cared about Kyle and had worried about him from the time he'd become his assistant. He wanted more from their association than what existed between them. He wanted a brother, but he also wanted Kyle to be happy and to find some peace. Perhaps Tamara could help Kyle heal.

Maybe he was some crazy mixed-up individual. And here he was trying to solve Kyle's problems when he needed help himself.

Each night he thanked God for the person he'd become. The odds had been against him, but he'd beaten them and he'd done well for himself.

But he felt there was something in his life he still had to do. He'd been thinking seriously about it and needed to do it. He'd go to see his mother. He'd never been to see her since she had allowed the drugs to seep slowly into her mind and wreck their home. Now he felt he needed to see her so that he could move on without any burdens from his past dragging him down. He had a week before the appointment so he still had some time to make a decision. He wondered why, after all these years in prison, she finally wanted to see him.

He headed to the kitchen, turned the light on and searched for the number Tamara had given him. Then he remembered he'd placed it on a magnetic notepad on the refrigerator.

Finding the number, he dialed it and waited.

She answered on the fourth ring, but before he heard a voice, he heard giggling.

Then Tamara's voice came on the line. He could hear laughter in the background.

"It's Jared," he said. "I was wondering if you'd seen Kyle."

"Yes, he's over here. I invited him for dinner. Hold on, I'll put him on."

"Thank you," Jared said.

There was more giggling.

"What's up, bro?"

"I'm fine. Just got home and wondered where you were."

"I'll be home in a while. Tamara will bring me over."

Jared heard Tamara's voice in the background.

"Actually, Jared. I'll be staying over here to-night," Kyle said. The man sounded embarrassed, Jared thought.

"Kyle, that's cool. I'll see you in the morning. Sleep well," he teased.

"I definitely will," Kyle replied.

Jared put the phone down and smiled. Damn, Kyle was getting some. He laughed. Not that he was surprised. He'd recognized the signs, but he hadn't really expected things to happen so fast.

Well, it was the perfect night to do some study-ing and then he'd get a good night's rest.

His university life in Barbados was coming to an end for a while and he was looking forward to working in his field before he went on to complete his doctoral degree. But he wasn't sure what to do. Kyle had depended on him for the past five years. If he were to work in his field, he'd have to leave. Kyle would have to find someone else to take care of him.

It wasn't that he didn't want anyone else to take

his position. The fact was he didn't want to leave the house. He enjoyed living there despite his strange relationship with Kyle. This house was the only real home he'd known in years.

During the night, Kyle made love to Tamara again and again, until they'd fallen fast asleep. As the sun rose on the distant horizon, she realized that she'd fallen in love with Kyle Austin.

It was no sudden, stunning revelation, just a simple acceptance of what she'd known all along would be inevitable.

She'd fallen hopelessly in love with him.

She turned around from her spot at the window and watched him as he lay asleep on her bed. His arms were now wrapped around a pillow in the same way they'd been wrapped around her earlier.

She'd enjoyed their lovemaking. She still felt a warmth inside her hours after their session of hot, sweaty, scream-out-loud sex. Afterwards, he'd pulled her close to him and fallen asleep.

As she watched him, he turned and the covers shifted to reveal his naked form. She would never tire of seeing him. As she watched, his penis stirred and she smiled. She hoped he was dreaming of her.

She headed to the bed and lay down beside him. He pulled her to him again.

"You up already? What time is it?" he asked.

"It's just after six. You want to go running with me?"

He hesitated.

"If you're game, but I'd have to go get some clothes. You mind if Jared joins us?" he said after a moment.

"Sure, that would be fine. I'm just wondering if he hasn't left already."

"Nah, he usually goes at six-thirty," Kyle said.

"Okay, let's go," she said cheerfully.

Fifteen minutes later, dressed and in gear, Tamara and Jared started a slow jog, making sure that Kyle was comfortable. Five minutes later, they reached the large pasture where they could run without any obstructions. They kept a steady pace, circling the pasture for almost an hour.

Much later, they sat eating snow cones from the vendor whose cart was constantly surrounded by crowds of people, hoping for relief from the heat of the already-powerful sun.

"Thanks, I really enjoyed that," Kyle said. "We must do this again sometime. Not every day though. I wouldn't want to be a burden. I'd slow you down, but whenever it's good for you," he said.

"Kyle, it wouldn't be a problem any time. You can come run with me every morning if you wish. I'll be glad for the company," Jared said.

"Sorry, gentlemen, but I have to get going to feed my animals," Tamara said.

"I'm ready to go as soon as you are, but I can't run another step. So I'm hoping we're walking back," Jared said.

"I'm with you," Tamara responded. "I just want to walk back, have a shower and a light breakfast."

"You can join us for breakfast," Kyle said in invitation.

"Sorry," she replied, "I really have to get back to feed the animals and I have so much work to do today."

"Okay, fine, but you must come over tonight. You can join Kyle and me in watching a movie. I just got Forest Whitaker's new movie—the one he won that award for," Jared said.

"Okay, I promise I'll be over. Want me to bring anything?"

"No, I'll order a couple of pizzas," Kyle said.

"I'll bring a bottle of wine and a pitcher of my specially made lemonade," she insisted.

"Good, you can come over around eight, if that's fine with you," Kyle said.

"It's perfectly fine. I'll be there," Tamara said, her face beaming with a radiant smile.

Chapter 8

When Kyle woke Sunday morning in an empty bed, it felt strange. For the past few nights he'd slept over at Tamara's. He preferred to do his lovemaking to Tamara out of range of Jared's ears.

He'd already had to endure Jared's sly barbs, but he'd been too happy to care much about it.

Besides, Jared's wisecracks were the least of his problems. He had promised Tamara that he would visit with her family today. And the thought of facing her brothers had tied his stomach in knots. He wasn't sure if he was doing the right thing, but Tamara had convinced him that Shayne would be glad to have him over.

This would be the first time in five years that he'd mingled with a large number of people socially. When Tamara had called and told him that George and Troy were going to be at Shayne's as well, he'd been delighted. He remembered how fun it had been to be around the three friends at school. They'd accepted him for who he was. It hadn't mattered that his mother was dead. They'd treated him as if he were one of them. At one point they'd even invited him to be a part of the group. He would have made the fourth musketeer, but he'd turned the invitation down. He'd started to make a name for himself as a cricketer and he'd moved on to other friends. Now, on reflection, he realized he'd been so caught up in the superficial lifestyle of a star athlete that he'd missed out on some very meaningful friendships. His five years of solitude had been evidence of the lack of real relationships in his life. He'd had to deal with the accident and its aftermath all by himself.

He decided to get out of bed when he heard a knock on his door.

"Come in," he responded.

"Morning, Kyle. You need any help with anything? It's only eight o'clock so we have a few hours before we leave. Tamara called to say she would collect us about noon," Jared said.

"No, thanks. You already set out my clothes. I'll take a shower and be downstairs in a minute."

"Breakfast is done, so come down when you're ready. I'll be in the study doing some work," the younger man said.

When Jared left, Kyle took his time getting ready. As he moved downstairs, the delicious scent of scrambled eggs beckoned him.

Jared knew that meal was his favorite.

He walked into the kitchen, sat in his usual chair and gobbled his breakfast down. He carefully poured hot water and made himself a cup of tea, which he took with him into the sitting room. He didn't come here too often, but he wanted to relax and wait until it was time for them to leave. He'd listen to his audio version of Harry Potter's latest adventure while he waited.

But he couldn't focus on the story. His thoughts were too caught up in the upcoming events for that day.

Five years. Five years he'd kept himself hidden from the world like a hermit. He wondered how much of his life he'd let pass him by. He'd refused to learn Braille. He'd refused to go out. He'd even refused to join a support group for blind people.

Now, as he looked back on the five years, he realized that there was so much he could have done. There was so much he could still do. Maybe today was a step in the right direction. He didn't want to rush and do anything he would regret, so he planned on taking his time. But he did intend to make some changes in his life, he thought with determination.

Today he was a toddler about to take his first step, and it felt scary. But Kyle was determined to keep his fears to himself. He'd get in that car and head over to Shayne's home and it'd be as if nothing had changed. He'd smile and laugh and everyone would think he'd adapted to his blindness.

Little would they know he was a sniveling coward who'd hidden away, afraid of the world, for years.

He tried to think of all of the blind people who seemed to live normal, productive lives. Look at Stevie Wonder, Kyle thought to himself. There was a successful black man who'd made it big despite being blind.

He'd also made it big since his accident. After all, he'd sold a book that was an international best seller. His current advance spoke for itself.

He should have been proud of himself, but instead he'd wallowed in self-pity.

Well, things were going to change. And not just because of Tamara. Things would change because he wanted them to change.

He heard footsteps.

"What are you doing?" Jared asked.

"Nothing," Kyle said.

"You okay about today?"

"Yeah, I'm cool," Kyle replied. "Nothing to be worried about."

"It's alright to be apprehensive. It's your first time out in company," Jared said gently.

"I said I'm going to be alright!" he shouted. Immediately, he regretted his outburst. "I'm sorry," he said. "I didn't mean to shout at you."

"It's okay. I'm heading back to the study. I didn't mean to disturb you," Jared said.

"Don't go." Kyle said the two words with obvious difficulty.

Jared didn't say anything. Kyle could feel his presence, but nothing else.

"I didn't mean to say what I did. I'm sorry," Kyle said again.

"It's okay." For the first time, Kyle didn't hear the Jared he'd grown accustomed to. The younger man now sounded wary.

"I'm scared," he blurted out. "I haven't been out of this house much in the last five years. I haven't seen Shayne in more than ten. I wish they didn't have to see me like this. How am I going to feel with all those eyes staring at me? Kyle Austin, the former West Indian cricketer and playboy. Now nothing," Kyle said bitterly.

"Kyle, come off it. What craziness you talkin' 'bout?" Jared said. He sounded angry. "You've achieved more than most people have in a lifetime."

"So I have a best seller. I have millions, but I have no friends. And I'm blind, unable to do most things for myself."

"But that's no one's fault but yours. You push people away, so how do you expect to have friends?" Jared said.

"I push people away?" he asked, but the truth of the statement slammed him full force in the body. "I push people away, do I? I don't push *you* away," Kyle said.

"I'm just an employee, so I don't count." Kyle heard the hurt in Jared's voice.

"You do, Jared. You do count." Words rushed around in his head. He knew what he wanted to say, but he wasn't sure how to say it.

"Listen, I know I've not been the nicest person over the years, but you're important to me. It may seem that I only need you as an employee, but to be honest, I don't know how I'd have survived without you. I'm blind and there are so many things I can't do for myself. And not once have you complained."

"I had no need to. You've been paying me well," Jared said.

"Yes, I know, but it's about time our relationship moved beyond this…distance. Yes, you work for me, but it's about time I looked beyond that. We can still be friends, can't we?"

Again, there was silence. He was not surprised.

He'd not been the kindest person to Jared, but he'd made sure he had a good education without having to worry about meals or a place to live.

Unfortunately, he had not provided much of a home.

"That's fine with me, bro," Jared said finally.

"Good, so we'll go have a great lunch?"

"Yeah, sure. No need to worry, you'll be alright," Jared said.

Jared and Kyle spent the next hour or so watching and listening to a movie. Though they were both silent, a subtle warmth permeated the air. Things were definitely changing.

At exactly midday, Tamara's car pulled up in front of the massive entrance to the Knight Plantation. The door opened and her nephew Darius raced out of the house. He stopped when first Jared and then Kyle exited the car. After the briefest of moments, his gaze returned to Tamara and he jumped down the step and to her side.

"So how's my favorite nephew?" she asked, ruffling his hair.

"I'm your only nephew, Auntie Tam."

"Okay, smart one, where's your mom and dad?"

"Mom's in the kitchen and Dad's in the garden."

His gaze turned to Kyle.

"You're Uncle Kyle? Daddy tells me that I must

call you that because you are his good friend." And then his voice went soft. "You can take my hand and I'll take you into the house. My daddy tells me you can't see, but I'm not to say anything about it." And with that he put his small hand into Kyle's larger one.

"I'll walk slowly since my dad tells me I do everything too fast," he said.

Tamara smiled as she watched her nephew lead Kyle into the house. She glanced at Jared, who looked a bit worried.

"Jared, there is no need to worry. Darius will take good care of Kyle," she told him.

"I can see that Kyle's in good hands," Jared replied.

Walking up the steps, they entered the house. Tamara never ceased to be amazed at the beauty and grandeur of her childhood home. She was heading in the direction of the kitchen when she saw her brother heading toward them.

Immediately, he hugged Tamara and shook Jared's hand when she introduced him.

"I just spoke to Kyle briefly before Darius took him to meet Carla. I'm assuming they'll end up in the dining room where George and Troy are. Gladys should be on her way down soon. I'm just going to get a few bottles of wine from the cellar. I'll be back up in a minute," he said.

Tamara watched as her brother walked away.

He was too handsome for his own good. She remembered how she showed him off to her friends at school.

Now he was married, with a wonderful wife and a healthy son, another child on the way.

"Let's go to the kitchen so I can introduce you to Carla first and then we'll join the men in the dining room."

She wondered how Kyle was doing. She knew he was trying to be brave.

There was not much she could do about it right now. For the moment, he was on his own.

When Darius had taken his hand and walked him slowly into the house, Kyle had felt like racing back to the familiarity of Jared's support. He'd counted to ten and willed himself to follow the little boy who'd kept up a steady conversation about everything and nothing. By the time he reached the kitchen, where Carla Knight seemed to be cooking up a heavenly feast, Kyle had decided he was taking the little boy home with him.

"Mommy, this is Daddy's friend, Uncle Kyle. He was one of the bestest cricketers." He then added in a whisper, "But he can't see anymore, so we're not supposed to talk about it."

He heard Carla's husky laughter.

"I see you've met my precocious li'l darling.

Kyle, it's a pleasure to have you over. I've heard so much about you," she said. He could tell from her accent that she wasn't Barbadian. She spoke with a distinct American accent.

"Thanks for inviting me over," he said.

"Kyle, you're welcome here any time. Shayne made it quite clear you're family," she told him. "I'll let Darius take you to Shayne and the others. I'll be finished in a bit. Where are Tamara and your friend…Jared? I think that's the name Tamara gave us."

"They're on the way, Mommy. I'll take Uncle Kyle to Uncle George and Uncle Troy," Darius said.

"That's a good boy," Clara said to her son.

"Nice to meet you, Clara," Kyle said as Darius tugged him away.

They walked along a long hallway before he heard voices and laughter.

"You're going to turn here, Uncle Kyle, and we'll be in the living room. Uncle George, Uncle Troy, here is Uncle Kyle," Darius said by way of an introduction.

"Thanks, Darius. Good afternoon, all," Kyle said to the room of people.

"So he's going to call us 'all,'" George said, his voice filled with laughter. "As if we weren't the best of friends at school."

"Yeah, George. Long time no see," Kyle said.

"So you know the voice and can make fun of yourself. Good, you haven't changed that much. Come here, man. Give me a hug," George said in his booming voice.

Before he could protest, Kyle felt two large arms embrace him tightly.

So, George was still short, he thought.

"Damn, Kyle, it's so good to see you. I wondered about you, but no one seemed to know where you'd disappeared to. I assumed you were in the States," he said.

"Okay, okay, don't let's all get teary eyed now," another voice said. Kyle felt George's arms move away and then Troy, many inches taller, enfolded him in another tight hug.

"I second George. You're going to have to tell us what we did to deserve this treatment for five years. I know we weren't as close after you started playing cricket, but you were our friend," Troy said.

"Is it alright to say I'm sorry? I've had to deal with so many things. Losing my sight was rough, but I'm much better now. I'm learning to cope. Even more so, thanks to Tamara. You'll meet my assistant Jared soon, too," Kyle said.

"You're forgiven. It's just good to see you again. And look at it this way. At least you don't have to see George's ugly mug."

"Troy, you're lucky our godson is here. Other-

wise, I'd have a few prime words for you,"
George said.

Before Troy could reply, Darius shouted,
"Daddy! Daddy!"

And for the third time he felt a pair of strong
arms surround him. "Kyle, it's been too long. I
couldn't believe it when Tamara told me you lived
just next door to her. I had to promise her I'd wait
until today to see you."

"Yeah," Troy said. "We were planning to storm
your house the same night Shayne told us."

"Come, come, sit," Shayne said.

"I'll take him to the chair, Dad. I'll put him in
the chair right here."

"Thanks, Darius. You're such a good boy."

"I know, Daddy. You tell me all the time,"
Darius said as he looked adoringly at his father.

And then Kyle heard Carla's voice.

"It's time for lunch. Gladys and I just added the
finishing touches, so if everyone is ready to eat,
follow me to the dining room. Oh, and I forgot to
introduce this handsome young man here with
Tamara. This is Jared. He's Kyle's assistant—
which means he's family," she said.

"Well, I'm hungry, all," Shayne said. "Go,
Darius. You can lead the guests to the dining room.
I'll take care of Kyle."

It felt strange to feel his arm in the strong,

muscular hand of his former schoolmate, and the unexpected squeeze made him feel kind of strange and emotional inside.

During the walk to the dining room, Shayne politely asked him what he had been doing with his time. Kyle told him about his writing.

"Okay, we're in the dining room now. You can sit here between Darius and me. Of course, his mother will sit next to him so he won't spill everything on his plate," Shayne said.

Kyle felt a rush of apprehension. But Shayne immediately eased his fear.

"You just tell me what I have to do for you and I'm sure we'll be alright," Shayne said.

Kyle stretched his hand forward and touched the back of the chair. He pulled it out and sat. At least he could do something for himself.

Briefly, Shayne told him what was on the table and filled a plate for him with the foods that Kyle requested.

As he ate, Kyle listened to the conversation around him. It seemed as if everyone was trying to talk at the same time.

And then the strangest thing happened. He felt his body relax. The tension went away and he felt good. He felt at home. He'd been in this house many times in his early teens and he'd loved the sense of warmth that filled the home.

When Shayne's parents had passed away, he'd been on tour with the cricket team in Australia. He'd sent a card, but he'd never really reached out to his friend. To say they'd lost touch was an understatement. He'd deserted his friends. He knew he didn't deserve to be here, but he wanted to be here all the same.

He had every intention of enjoying himself and he knew he would.

That night, his arms around the woman he was falling in love with, Kyle reflected on the day he'd had.

In the late evening, when the chill of the ocean breeze cooled the land of the day's heat, Shayne had pulled him away from his new friend Darius.

He'd taken Kyle to the stable to meet his horses. He'd met the horses and Prince had nuzzled him and he'd almost found himself transported back in the past.

"Kyle," Shayne said, "why?"

Kyle knew exactly what he meant.

"I don't know," he replied. "I just got all caught up in the cricket fever. I lost myself along the way. Here I was, a little island boy, living his greatest dream and making lots of money to boot. Women were clinging to me and I had the world in my hands," Kyle said, trying to explain.

"But what about after the accident? You could have called me, George, Troy. We were your friends."

"I'm sorry, Shayne. I know I fouled up, but after the accident I really wasn't sure how to act." He cringed at how pitiful he sounded.

"Damn, Kyle, I'm sorry. I didn't mean to be insensitive. It's just that when I read about the accident I went out of my mind with worry. We even tried to get in contact with you, but it was as if you'd fallen off the face of the earth."

"I think that is what I tried to do. To be honest, this is the first time in years I've ventured so far away from home," Kyle confessed.

"You must be kidding, Kyle."

"No, I'm not. I hired Jared to do most things for me. And I have a housekeeper who comes in every day to cook and clean."

"That's good, but you need someone you can talk to," Shayne said.

"You're right, Shayne. Tamara has made me realize that I've truly neglected a part of me."

"And what part is that?"

"I've lost my independent spirit. Instead of dealing with my blindness, I tried to hide away in the country and forget that there's a world out there that I'm still very much a part of."

"Maybe you just dealt with it the best way you could."

"Maybe, but I don't think so. I'm blind and don't even know how to read Braille. When I realized I was blind I refused to learn anything. I had the money so I hired someone to do everything for me," Kyle said.

"I see what you mean. But the fact that you're here means you're doing something about it."

"Yeah, I am."

There was silence, then Shayne asked, "So what are your intentions for my sister?"

"Not that it's any business of yours," Kyle said, but smiled. "I'm not sure. I like her. She makes me feel alive in a way I haven't felt for years. Do I want to marry her? I don't know. I'm not sure any woman would want to marry a man who's blind. I'm not even sure how she feels about me. I wonder at times if I'm not one of those strays she feels sorry for."

When Shayne responded, his answer was very clear. "Just promise me you won't hurt her."

"I promise. But can you promise she won't hurt me?"

In the middle of the night, Tamara turned toward him, her body perfect against his. His erection strained, jerking with its need for her.

She grasped him in her hand, sending a shiver through his body as he gave in to the pleasure of wanting her.

She turned him, forcing him to lie on his back.

He felt the tentative touch of her lips on him and then she took him in her mouth, performing a gentle suction that caused him to moan with pleasure.

When her mouth left him, he stifled his groan of protest. Her hand touched his throbbing penis again and he heard the familiar tearing of foil and then her hands rolling the condom onto him.

Before he could reach for her and move above her, he felt her on him until the deep warmth of her enveloped him.

Above him, she started a tantalizing movement, up and down, up and down.

He joined her, thrusting his hips upward to meet her, loving the silky, tight feel of her.

But he ached to take control, wanted to pleasure her, too. At that moment, Kyle realized he was experiencing the essence of love.

In his younger days, he'd always been the one in control during sex. He was the man. But now he realized that was not love, it was ownership. He wanted what he had with Tamara to be different and special.

So he continued to let her take control, feeling her hips grind against him.

And as she moved up and down, he felt the first glimmer of his climax.

His toes curled and his body contracted and he felt the blood pumping through his penis. The sensations were so intense they made him want to scream at the top of his voice.

And when the light flashed within his head and he gave in to that sweet familiar rush of pleasure, he screamed—a loud, free sound that came from deep within his soul. He knew somehow that he wanted to experience this explosive passion with Tamara every day of his life.

When Tamara collapsed on him, he drew her closer, and knew beyond a shadow of doubt that he loved this woman more than life itself.

How was he ever going to convince her that she should spend the rest of her life with him?

Jared smiled. He'd enjoyed the day. The lunch and the fun they'd had after had made the day perfect.

He'd not talked much, but he had savored the company of the Knight family. And he'd been made to feel like a part of the family. Not for one moment had he felt like an outsider. Shayne and Carla, George and Troy, and even young Darius, had made him feel completely at home.

He'd even felt more special when Carla had made the official announcement that she was pregnant with her and Shayne's second child.

He'd looked at both of them with awe. Jared hoped that someday he would have that same love for himself.

His thoughts strayed to his family. His scheduled visit with his mother was only a few hours away and he still hadn't decided if he was going to see her.

He didn't want to go, but he could not deny his curiosity or his overwhelming need to see what had become of his mother. His memories were of a pretty, fragile woman who allowed every man willing to support her and her son into her bed. In spite of all that had happened he'd never doubted that his mother loved him.

So maybe he owed her that much. He'd go. He'd see her and once and for all purge the image of her from his tortured mind.

Chapter 9

The next few days were uneventful and peaceful
as Tamara and Kyle got into a comfortable routine.

During the day, they'd explore the surrounding
area. At night they would watch television. Sometimes they would watch with Jared at Kyle's house.
At other times, Kyle and Tamara would spend the
night at her place. On those nights, the evening's
viewings always ended in lovemaking.

Tamara gave herself a mental shake and tried to
focus on the day ahead. Today she wanted to go to
the Sheraton Mall in the south of the island. She
hated to go into the city with its noise and constant
flow of traffic, but she needed to get her gifts

for Christmas. She had every intention of getting something for Kyle, but she hadn't decided what she would get. Maybe she'd see something she liked for him at the mall.

In the middle of the night, when he'd fallen asleep and she lay wrapped in his arms, she'd finally admitted to her feelings.

She was truly in love with Kyle Austin.

From the day Tamara had met him, she'd felt a rush of unexpected emotion. Now she knew what it was.

The thought scared her. She wasn't even sure if she wanted to be committed to a man at this point in her life. She eventually wanted to get married, have a bundle of kids and a handsome, loving husband. But for now, she was content with her career…and her animals.

But loving someone didn't mean he was the perfect person to spend her life with.

First of all, his blindness would be a problem. Not that she had a problem with marrying a blind man, but she wasn't sure she wanted to deal with a man who couldn't accept his blindness.

At least Tamara had noticed some changes in Kyle's attitude lately. His agreement to visit Shayne suggested that he was ready to move on with his life.

One thing that remained a problem for her was Kyle's attitude toward Christmas. It seemed so unnatural to her. She'd always seen this time of year as a time for family and friends, but most of all, it was time to reflect on the most significant aspect of the season—the celebration of the birth of Christ.

So what was she going to do?

She didn't think that saying anything to him would make a difference. What she needed to do was show Kyle the spirit of Christmas. Show him that there were positive things about the holiday.

Then maybe his whole negative attitude toward the season would dissipate.

Kyle entered the study and moved to his computer. He planned to dictate the next chapter of his new book. His imaginary hero had finally revealed his story to Kyle. Kyle wanted to get his thoughts down before the inspiration passed.

Kyle never ceased to be amazed by how his creative mind worked. At first he'd thought that his dive into the literary world of the imagination had been a fluke. He couldn't even remember what had motivated him to write, but he did remember waking to images of a movie playing in his mind and stories unfolding in his head. At first he'd thought he was going crazy.

When Jared had returned home from classes that night he'd reluctantly told the young man about the story.

The rest was history. Jared had told him that he loved it and that he would check out the technology that would allow Kyle to dictate the story. Jared had essentially taken care of everything.

Of course, Kyle had increased Jared's salary, something the young man had refused.

Little did Jared know that he'd created an account for him and placed the extra money into it. He'd planned to tell Jared about the fund when his master's program was over. Kyle knew that Jared wanted to go to England to finish his education. There was more than enough in the fund to cover Jared's expenses and tuition.

Jared would soon be going to England. Kyle still panicked when he thought of that inevitability. Whether it was for studying or marriage, Kyle knew that Jared would eventually move on.

An unexpected wave of sadness washed over him. He was forced to admit he cared about the boy. They had so much in common.

Years ago, one Christmas, he'd asked God to give him a brother and he'd been so angry when his mother never got pregnant. Instead, she'd died. Of course, he'd blamed God and that had been another strike against Christmas and all things religious.

Now, in some ironic twist of fate, he had someone who represented the brother he'd dreamed about all those years ago. And he'd refused to acknowledge him as such.

Over the years he'd watched Jared's academic progress and felt an overwhelming sense of pride. Of course, he'd always rewarded him with something tangible, but not once had he told Jared how proud he was of him.

That was the kind of insensitive person he'd become. He'd been selfish. Despite his treatment, Jared had stayed with him and gone beyond the call of duty.

He remembered once when he'd taken ill. Each time he'd awakened, Jared had been there. And each time his body had trembled and shivered, he'd felt the firm, comforting touch of someone who cared about him.

Damn. Had his hatred for Christmas and his disgust at what God had done to him turned him into a monster?

There was so much in his life he needed to straighten out. And he would start right now. Kyle decided there and then to buy Jared a gift.

He'd learned so much about himself in the past few weeks. The most important discovery was that he had an overwhelming capacity for love.

Kyle's hands moved across the surface of the computer, finding the headphones and microphone he'd left there more than a week ago. If he was to meet his deadline he really should be spending more time here, but of course, he'd been distracted.

So for the next hour or so, he'd push everything but Nkosi's story from his mind.

There would be time later to think of what he'd get Tamara, Jared and Ms. Simpson for Christmas. And of course, he couldn't forget Shayne and his family, plus George and Troy.

Jared sighed as he entered the room where he'd be meeting with his mother. The journey to the prison in the north of the island had been a long one. He'd found comfort in the music of the season, soothing with its odes to joy and peace to all mankind.

But inside, his heart beat rapidly and he wondered what kind of meeting this was going to be.

The door opened and his mother entered, her hands cuffed behind her back, being escorted by an officer.

All Jared could do was continue to stare at her.

The woman who stood before him was nothing like what he'd expected. The ten years of incarceration had really changed her. Instead of the drugged-out woman he'd expected, the person who sat before him seemed to be a proud woman. She held her head high and looked at him with confidence. But when he looked at her closely, he caught a glimpse of sadness in her eyes.

"I'm glad you came, Jared."

He didn't speak, just nodded.

"Boy, you've grown. And you're so handsome," she said. Her voice sounded choked. It was filled with anguish.

She smiled, a glimpse of happiness that reached her eyes.

"So what are you doing? Are you working?"

"Not yet. I'm studying at the university," Jared said.

"You are?" She sounded surprised. "What are you studying?"

"I'm getting a master's in psychology."

"I'm so proud of you. My son's getting his master's," she said as if she expected the walls to respond. The officer nodded, his expression remaining bland.

"So what have you been doing?" It was a silly question but he really didn't know what else to say. What did you ask someone who'd been in prison for the past ten years? Jared wondered.

"Oh, nothing much. There is a program here that allows you to do the regional exams. I did a few over the years and passed. But let's not talk about me. Tell me about yourself. Are you married?"

"No, I'm not. I've been focusing on my studies. There'll be time for that later," Jared said.

"So you want to get married?"

"I'm not sure. Maybe. There was a girl once. But I let her go," he said. "That was a long time ago."

"My boy, that's one thing you don't do. Never let a good woman go. You may never be lucky to find another one."

She glanced at the clock above him.

"Well, my fifteen minutes are up. I'm glad you came. Maybe you can come again."

"We'll see," he replied.

"Don't worry that I'm in here. I've been doing well. Have a blessed Christmas."

"You, too," Jared said.

For the briefest of moments he felt the urge to hug her, but knew he couldn't.

He just watched her walk away and knew he'd be back.

Jared drove along the ABC highway. He'd just passed the St. James Parish Church. The rain was drizzling but he had no difficulty in seeing where he was going.

He tried not to focus on his mother. The meeting with her had left him drained, but he was still proud at how he'd handled it.

Behind him a truck was trying to overtake him, but he paid no attention to it. Ahead he saw the headlights of an oncoming car at the same time the truck tried to pass him again. He slowed his car, hoping the truck would be able to overtake his car. Instead he heard a high screech and a loud bang. Then he saw a pair of headlights coming directly toward him. He instinctively swerved, causing his car to skid, and suddenly he was airborne. When his car landed, it was headed straight for the concrete embankment.

The last thing he saw before he lost consciousness was his mother reaching out to him and hugging him.

Kyle received the call at 11:30 p.m.

A stiff, professional voice told him that his brother Jared had been in an accident and he needed to get to the hospital.

He listened for the disconnection and then dialed Tamara's number.

No reply.

He needed to go next door and find her.

Tamara was wrapping the final Christmas gift when she heard a knock on her door followed by a voice.

Kyle?

What was he doing here at this time?

She jumped up and raced to the door.

When she opened it, he stood facing the building, his cane searching for the step, the look on his face one of intense determination.

"What's wrong, Kyle?"

"It's Jared. He's been in an accident. I need someone to take me to the hospital."

"Stay here. I'll be right back."

Tamara rushed up the stairs, took off what she was wearing and slipped into a T-shirt and pair of jeans.

She moved quickly down the stairs and out the door, closing it behind her.

"I'm ready," she said and took his cane. She then took his hand and led him to the car, seating him before she moved to the driver's side and got in.

A few minutes later, the car was speeding along the highway, heading to the hospital in the city.

For a while they traveled in silence.

"He's going to be fine, Kyle."

"How do you know that? How do you know he's going to be alright?"

"I just know. God's not going to let anything happen to him," Tamara assured him.

"Hasn't God already allowed something to happen? A week before Christmas and this happens. And just when I was beginning to think that I was being silly about the season. Just another nightmarish memory to add to all the ones that have come before."

"Kyle, you're being irrational. Things like this

happen all year round. It has nothing to do with Christmas."

"Can we just not talk about this Christmas thing right now? We're here arguing about Christmas and Jared may be dying," Kyle said bitterly.

With that he turned his face away from her, as if he could see the houses and cane fields that flashed by.

Twenty minutes later, when they arrived at the hospital, Kyle stepped from the car before Tamara could assist him. She closed the door and reached for his hand as they headed to the emergency room.

On arriving, they were told that Jared had been sent up to one of the wards.

When they arrived at the ward, they were taken immediately to see him. Kyle had come prepared and in a short while they'd made arrangements for Jared to be transferred to a private room.

They sat in the waiting room as Jared was moved to his new room.

"I'm sorry. I didn't mean to be rude. I was just worried about Jared," he said. He felt guilty because Tamara was always so kind to him and he repaid her kindness by snapping at her. She deserved better from him, Kyle thought.

"I understand, but you need to do something about

your temper. You have a habit of biting my head off when you get annoyed," Tamara said quietly.

"Yeah, I do have a habit of doing that. And I'm really sorry. I'm trying."

"I've noticed," she replied, the sarcasm evident in her tone.

"You know, today I finally decided to give Christmas a chance again. I even thought about buying gifts and now this happens," Kyle said.

"Kyle, you know that the decision you made was the correct one. Don't let this change your mind about Christmas. At least see Jared before you go all ballistic," Tamara replied.

As he was about to respond, Tamara heard footsteps along the corridor. She jumped up when a doctor came in their direction.

He stopped when he reached them. "You're Jared's brother?" he asked, speaking directly to Kyle.

"Yes, I am," Kyle said.

"Mr. Austin, Jared is going to be fine. He sustained some minor injuries, but we want to keep him overnight to make sure he's totally alright. He'll be in a bit of pain because he bruised a few ribs. Fortunately, he was wearing a seat belt so it was not as bad as it could have been. We've given him a mild sedative, and I'm sure he'll feel a bit better in the morning. I'll take you to see him."

With that, the doctor turned and stopped, waiting for them to follow him.

Tamara put her arms around Kyle.

"At least it seems like Jared's doing better than they originally thought," Tamara said.

When they reached Jared's room, Tamara and Kyle entered cautiously, still expecting the worst. Of course, Kyle would be spared seeing any problems with Jared's appearance.

Jared lay on the stark white sheets, asleep. The gentle rise and fall of his chest was a welcome sight.

Tamara sighed in relief.

"Is he okay? Does he look okay?" Kyle asked.

"He looks a bit battered, but he seems fine. And he's breathing easily," Tamara said.

"Good. I hope there's nothing seriously wrong. I don't have much trust in doctors."

"He'll be fine, Kyle. You have to be positive."

"My experience with accidents has not been positive, but I agree. I need to be positive for him," Kyle conceded.

"You can sit here in this chair next to the bed if you like."

Kyle stretched out his cane, reaching for the chair before he lowered himself into it.

"Where is the bed? Can I touch him?"

"Stretch your hand forward. He's just in front of you."

Tamara watched as Kyle extended his hand forward and touched Jared. His hand searched until he found Jared's hand.

He held it.

"You think God will hear me if I pray?" Kyle asked.

"I'm sure he will," Tamara replied. "He's always listening."

"I'm sure he hasn't heard me in a while, since I've not had anything to ask. Will you pray with me?"

"Yes," she replied. "I will."

Tamara reached her hand out and held Kyle's free hand, feeling a warmth spread inside her when he squeezed it.

"You mind staying here for a while? We can go home and come back early in the morning. I'll be fine if you can't."

"I can come with you. Everything is ready for Christmas and the office. I just planned to enjoy the rest of the season."

"This is not a great holiday for you. You're all set for Christmas and you end up being at the hospital all night," Kyle said.

"That's what friends are for, Kyle, and I consider Jared my friend."

There was silence for a while and then Kyle's voice came softly into the room.

"God, I haven't called on you much in my life, but

this isn't about me. I want you to take care of Jared. Whatever you have to do to make him live, then you do it. I remember enough to know that you said that if we ask, you'll give. Thank you," Kyle said.

Tamara squeezed his hand. She looked up at Kyle and realized there were tears in his eyes. She rose and stood behind the chair, her arms coming around him.

"I don't know what's happening to me, but I'm acting like a weepy old woman," he said as he brushed the tears from his face.

"No, Kyle, you're just learning to care about the people who care about you," Tamara said.

"You know that Jared and I just talked yesterday about our relationship. I realized I need to start treating him as a brother and not just as an employee."

"He worships the ground you walk on."

"Does he?"

"Yeah, he does. Why do you think he puts up with all your attitude? Taking care of you is so important to him because you're the only real family he knows. With his mother in prison and being raised in a foster home until he was sixteen, it means that you've provided him with the first real home he has ever had," she said.

Tamara watched as Kyle absorbed her words. His caring for Jared was written all over his face.

His concern warmed her heart. She slipped her arms from around him when a nurse quietly entered the room.

"I'm sorry, folks. Visiting hours are over. You can come back as early as eight o'clock in the morning tomorrow," she said.

"We'll be here," Kyle told her.

"If we need to, we'll call. I have your number on his file, Mr. Austin, but I'm sure he'll be alright," the nurse said.

"Thanks for taking care of him," Kyle said, and then turned to Tamara. "Are you ready to go?"

"Yes, let's go home and get some rest and be back early in the morning," she said as she led him out of the room.

Later that night, they lay in bed holding each other. Tamara felt good next to him, Kyle thought. He didn't want anything else tonight. To hold her would be enough.

She stirred in his arms.

"You okay?" she asked.

"I'm fine. I was thinking about how lucky I am. I'm lucky to have met you. I'm lucky because I still have good friends despite avoiding them for the past five years, and I'm lucky because I have Jared. How do you think he'd feel if I became his official guardian?"

"I'm sure he'd have no problem with that," Tamara said.

"I'd hire someone else to take care of me and let him get on with his life."

"Do you think he'd want that? Why couldn't you become his guardian, let him continue with his studying, but still let him live with you? I can help out in any way I can. Besides, now you sleep at my place most of the time," Tamara said.

"That's true. I've been thinking about talking to my lawyer about drawing up the papers. I'll let him know on Christmas. It'll be my gift to him."

"I'm sure he'd be happy," she said.

"I hope so. I've taken him for granted for too long."

There was silence.

"So can we talk about us after Jared is well?" Tamara asked quietly.

"Yeah, I promise we'll talk. For now we need to get some sleep," he said as he pulled her closer.

Hours later he awoke to the sound of screeching tires and a blinding pain in his head.

"You okay, honey?" Tamara asked.

"I'm alright. I was having a nightmare," he said.

"Were you dreaming about the accident?" she asked.

"Yeah, my accident. I haven't dreamt about it

in years. What happened to Jared must have triggered it. I'll be fine," he said.

She wrapped her arms around him again and he held on to her for dear life.

He wondered for the hundredth time whether they could have a future together. And for the first time he felt like it was really possible.

Oh, well, time enough to think about that, he thought. For now, it was all about getting Jared better. When that was over he'd spend time courting Tamara and convincing her that marriage to a blind man wouldn't be half-bad.

He closed his eyes, willing himself to sleep. And as he tried to drift off to sleep, he realized he was too aroused to rest. His awareness of her had him hot and erect. There was time enough to play, he thought. He was just about to tease her awake when the phone rang.

He reached for it on the nightstand.

"Hello?"

"Hey, Kyle, it's Shayne. I just heard the news about Jared. Is he okay?"

"Damn, I should have called," Kyle said. "Yeah, Shayne. The doctor said that Jared would be fine."

"Great," Shayne said with relief.

"How did you know about Jared?"

"I heard it on the evening news, but the reporter also mentioned that you were Jared's guardian.

The report mentioned you by name. I thought you should be prepared for the media blitz that will surely follow the revelation of your whereabouts," Shayne said.

"I didn't want that to happen. What am I going to do, Shayne? I don't want that kind of notoriety again," Kyle said.

"You know reporters. They see a story and they go crazy, but don't fret yourself. In a few weeks the story will die down and things will be back to normal," Shayne said.

"I hope so," Kyle said, his voice full of doubt.

"You take care of yourself. I'm assuming since my sister is not at her place she's over there with you. Can I speak to her?"

"She's sleeping. Want me to wake her up?"

"No, definitely not. No one wakes Tamara Knight."

"Okay, I'll tell her you called. And, Shayne, thanks for calling."

"No problem, bro. Jared is family now. Carla and I will go to the hospital tomorrow and visit. I'm sure Troy and George will come, too. I've let them know. But you said he's doing okay?"

"Yes, he's doing fine."

"Good, I'm glad. You have a good night," Shayne said.

"You, too."

"Oh, and we'll talk about you sleeping with my sister later. Of course, I have to find out what your intentions are," Shayne said, trying to keep his voice stern and serious. "If you want to ask me for it, I'll give you my blessing. Just make sure you don't hurt her."

"I promise you I won't. Now, I need to get some sleep. We want to be at the hospital early to be there when Jared wakes up."

"Then you get off to sleep. I'll see you some-time in the morning at the hospital," Shayne said.

"Thanks again, bro," Kyle responded.

"No problem," Shayne replied and hung up.

Kyle set the phone down. Tamara was still asleep. She must be really tired. He was feeling a bit weary, too, but he couldn't sleep.

He didn't know what was going to happen in his relationship with Tamara. Yes, he'd thought about marriage, but thinking about it didn't mean it would happen.

Jared was the closest he'd come to having a friend. At least he was until Tamara had come into his life. How would his relationship with Jared change if he married Tamara? he wondered.

It was strange for him to be even thinking about marriage.

When Chantal had rejected him, realizing that

his blindness was permanent, Kyle had decided that the institution was no longer a part of his future.

In fact, he'd realized that marrying Chantal would have been a mistake. Their relationship had not been based on any kind of love, but on good sex. And the fact that Chantal had been perfect for the image he'd been cultivating for the public. He didn't think that a marriage like that would have lasted.

And now he was back in the public eye.

Perhaps the press would just leave him be, but he knew that was only wishful thinking. The press in Barbados was no different from any other place. He only hoped that something a lot more interesting would soon return him to obscurity.

Of course, he had no intention of returning to his former lifestyle. One thing he did know was that he'd matured over the past five years. The accident had forced him to take a good look at where he had been heading and who he'd become.

Tamara groaned next to him.

He listened in the silence as she settled down. Soon her breathing was gentle and steady again.

He ached to make love to her, but he was beginning to feel the heaviness of sleep taking over him.

As he drifted into that magic land where heroes were perfect and never died, he experienced a sense of dread. He wondered if he'd be hero enough for Tamara. So far, he'd learned one thing—to love a Knight, he had to be much more of a man than he'd been.

Chapter 10

The next morning Tamara woke to the sound of the shower running. She jumped up, immediately remembering what had happened the night before. She took her watch off the dresser. Just before six o'clock. It was way too early for them to visit Jared.

She'd go next door shortly and take care of the animals before she left with Kyle for the hospital.

But thoughts of Kyle in the shower stirred something inside her.

She needed him.

She slipped out of the large T-shirt she wore and let it drop to the ground. When she entered the bathroom, she pulled the curtain back and stood staring at him, feeling the desire building inside.

She could look at him all day.

He immediately turned in her direction. She was growing accustomed to his eyes looking at her but not seeing her. There was no doubt that he was blind, but it didn't detract from his beauty.

She watched as his penis stirred, the erection coming quickly.

"So are you going to just stand there staring at me? It's unfair to have that visual advantage over me. I need to touch you," he said as he reached for her.

She didn't need to be told twice. Tamara joined Kyle in the shower. She stepped into his arms and placed her lips against his to received the kiss that would stir her until she begged for him to take her.

One thing she had learned about Kyle was that he used his hands, depending on his sense of touch, to give her pleasure. He made love to her with his hands, touching every part of her body until she tingled with excitement and anticipation.

And she loved the way he kissed, teasing her with his tongue and making her tremble.

His lips left her mouth, roaming all over her body and pleasuring her. She turned the faucet off as he stooped, moving down her body until he stopped at the core of her heat. His tongue continued to tantalize as she felt the rush of pleasure inside her.

She wanted him.

Kyle raised himself, finding her mouth again.

She felt the prodding of his erection at her entrance, and then he slipped inside her. She threw her head back, gasping for breath as he slowly pushed inch after inch inside her.

She pulled him close, shifting so that her back rested against the wall. He gripped her bottom, raising her. She instinctively wrapped her legs around his waist. When Kyle pulled out of her and then plunged back in again, she gloried at his full length and thickness.

She wrapped her legs tighter around him, feeling him pulse deep inside her.

For a while, she accepted the rhythm. Then he slowed the pace. The change created an intense ache inside and she reveled in his ability to pleasure her.

She placed her hand around his neck, still gripping him around the waist with her legs, urging him on. Kyle responded, increasing his pace until she felt like she was riding one of her horses.

And then the moment that she wished wouldn't come so soon began. Her body was aching for release and Kyle was giving her just what she needed.

It started with a slow build of heat and a spark of fire deep inside her. For a moment, she panicked. They'd made love before, but she'd never felt it like this. Her whole body felt on fire, every nerve of her body was alive.

When his body began to shake, she placed her mouth on his, wanting to capture some of his passion.

But she couldn't. Her body had a mind of its own. When release came, her body was prepared for the intensity of it, but her mind wasn't. She screamed as the waves of pleasure burst inside her. Hers was a joyous cry of pure elation.

When their bodies eventually relaxed, embracing the calm, she held him close.

"I love you, Kyle Austin," she said.

He didn't reply. He only placed his lips on hers and her words were lost in his kiss.

Long after Tamara had left to go feed the animals, Kyle sat in his office thinking about her. He'd hurt Tamara. He knew that much. When she told him she loved him, his heart had soared but his own words of love had remained stuck in his throat, locked there by fear.

He loved her and wanted to be with her. He'd even convinced himself that they could make it work and that his blindness would not be a reason for denying them a forever. And yet, he'd failed to tell her how he felt that morning. She'd offered him her love and he'd shut her out emotionally.

He wanted to spend his life with her. He wanted to touch her stomach when she was swollen with his child. But he was spoiling their chances for a relationship with his silly insecurities. If he had any sense, he'd go over to her house right now and tell her he loved her, but he was scared.

Kyle Austin, former cricketer, lover of anything in a skirt, had been reduced to a scared boy, afraid to admit his love and to make a commitment.

Actually, the truth of the matter was that Kyle was afraid of himself.

He heard a noise and turned his head in that direction.

It was Tamara. He didn't need sight to know it was her.

"Are you ready, Kyle? It's after eight."

He rose to his feet, waiting for her hands to hold his. When they did, he gripped them, pulling her toward him.

He held her tightly, knowing what to say, but not how to say it.

He sighed, willing himself to be the man he knew he could be.

"I love you, Tamara Knight," he said.

He felt her hesitation, her caution.

"And I'm not saying it because you said it. I'm saying it because I mean it. I mean it with all that I am," he said earnestly.

"So what took you so long? What are you afraid of?" she asked. It never failed to amaze him how she knew exactly what he was feeling.

"I'm afraid of not living up to your expectations. I'm afraid of not being a good husband. I'm blind. What kind of a father and husband can I be? I won't be able to see if my child's in danger. I won't even be able to *see* my own children," he said.

"Oh, Kyle, you're going to be a great father. You're the kindest, most generous man I know. Look what you've done for Jared. Darius met you for one day and he's already devoted to you. He wants to know when he's going to see Uncle Kyle again. What more proof do you need?"

Tamara was right. Why did he continue to put himself down? He kept acting as if he were the world's first blind man. The reality was that blind men and women had been married and been successful husbands and wives for hundreds of years. Maybe he just needed to let it go and deal with the situation as each day came.

"To be honest, Tamara, I think it's more about my being afraid of all that's been happening, but I'm going to take your advice. I'm going to stop worrying about things I can't control. I've never been in a relationship like this before. I just need to trust you. If you're willing to deal with me and all my issues, then we can see how it goes," he said.

"I'm so glad to hear you say that. Good, we'll talk. But for now, you have someone important who needs you more than I do. You need to get him better and up and about. Are you ready to leave for the hospital?"

"Yes, I am," he replied. "But it's not only me he needs, it's *us* he needs. We're a team."

"Fair enough. Let's get to the hospital," she said.

He felt her hand take his. She was soft. Always soft. He squeezed it, drawing comfort from her touch.

Half an hour later, they walked along the corridor that led to Jared's room, her touch still providing comfort.

Today was slightly different. He noticed things he hadn't the night before. The silence, the sterile smell of disinfectant, smells he'd hated ever since his accident.

When Tamara stopped briefly, he knew they'd reached Jared's room.

He heard the soft creak of the door and then Tamara's gentle tug.

"Jared, you're awake. How're you feeling? Are you in any pain?"

Kyle stepped forward, following her voice into the room.

"Hi, Jared. You okay, bro?" Kyle said in greeting to Jared.

"I'm cool, Kyle, Tamara. Yeah, my side hurts a bit, but I think I'll be alright." Jared's voice was strained.

"Did the doctor come see you this morning? Did he say anything about your recovery?" Tamara asked.

"He said that I'm going to be alright. I have a few bruised ribs, but I'm lucky. The car was totaled. It's a miracle I wasn't killed. I promised myself that the first Sunday I can get into church, I'm going to be there. I could be dead," Jared said.

"There's nothing at all wrong with thanking God," Tamara said and smiled.

"I know," Jared said, yawning loudly. His voice was beginning to sound tired and he was breathing a bit faster.

"Jared, we're going to leave you for a while so that you can get a bit of rest. We'll be back a little later," Kyle said as he took Tamara's hand to leave.

"But you don't have to…" Jared tried to protest, but then a bout of coughing rattled his chest. "Okay, I'll take a rest," he added slowly.

There was silence and then the gentle sound of snoring.

"Didn't take him long to fall asleep," Tamara remarked wryly.

"No, his body is still weak from the trauma. Although I feel a lot better since I've heard him talking. I'm assuming he looks better than he did last night," Kyle said.

"He definitely does, but he'll have a few scratches and scars. Nothing a bit of cocoa butter won't solve. Do you want to go have brunch at this tiny restaurant I know on the south coast? We can be back in an hour or two," Tamara said.

"That's a good idea. I'll call Shayne, give him an update on Jared's condition, and I'll let him know when it's a good time to visit," Kyle said.

Tamara was surprised that Kyle hadn't protested when she'd suggested going to eat. But during the drive to the restaurant owned by an old school friend, he was silent and contemplative. She knew what must be running through his mind. He was worried about being bothered by reporters.

"I'll be fine," Kyle said, his voice a mere whisper. "I want to do this. I'm surprised they weren't parked out at the hospital this morning. I suppose that eventually they'll get to me."

"You'll have to be able to stand a few weeks of being in the public eye, then you'll have nothing to be worried about. It won't take the press long to move on to the next story."

"I've made up my mind that it has to be done. I have no intention of living my life as a hermit anymore. I want to be doing things again. I want to go shopping. I want to go to the beach and splash in the waves. That's what I want for me now."

"Well, we're about to take your first step back into the world of the living. We're here."

When they entered the restaurant, the sound of Christmas music oozed from the surround-sound speakers. At first Kyle balked, but he forced himself to relax, remembering that his issue with the season was a state of mind that was not logical. His anti-Christmas feelings stemmed from trau-matic events in his past. He was determined to move past those feelings and the events that had caused them.

His hand still holding Tamara's, he followed her lead through the restaurant until they reached their table and were seated.

After the waitress—a woman with a pleasant, friendly voice—had taken their orders for drinks, Tamara read the menu for him.

"Thanks," he said when she was done. "Maybe it's time I think about learning Braille."

"The choice is really yours," she replied, but he could hear the approval in her voice. "If you'd like, I could find out where you could take classes."

"Thank you. That would be nice," he said. "I know there's a vibrant association for the blind on the island. I'm thinking about joining. I'm sure being around others who've had to deal with this situation would help me."

"I'm sure it will. Just don't try to take on more than you can manage all at once," Tamara warned.

"I won't. In the past few days I've thought a lot about what I want out of life and what I've achieved. I know there are a lot of things I need to come to grips with as they relate to my blindness, but I'm willing to learn," he said.

"That's good. I hope I didn't force you into doing this."

"No, but you opened my eyes…or should I say opened my ears to listen. So I've listened," he said.

"Good. I'm glad you did. The waitress is coming back," she said. "Do you want the brunch special?" Tamara asked.

"Definitely. Fish cakes are my favorite. And whatever they serve them with is fine by me," he said.

Tamara handed him his drink and gave the waitress their order before continuing the conversation.

"So you think you're going to be alright out in public?"

"I think so. Okay, I'm not sure, but I'm ready to deal with whatever happens."

"Good, because a reporter and cameraman are heading in our direction," she said.

Before the words were out of her mouth, a voice almost shouted at him.

"Mr. Austin, I have a few questions for you," the reporter said.

"Since you're the first reporter to come after me, I'm going to just say this and say it nicely. When you see me in public in the company of a beautiful lady, don't ever interrupt me. Is that understood?"

"Yes, sure, Mr. Austin."

"Good. Call me tonight at the number on this card and I'll give you an exclusive, but only if you'll leave me in peace."

"I promise," the reporter said. "Can I just get one photo for my article?"

"No problem. But after that, you go," Kyle said firmly.

He posed while the cameraman took the photo.

"You handled that quite well," Tamara said.

"I've decided that I'll deal with them personally. Give them the full scoop, and then they'll go away, I hope," he said.

At the same time, the waitress brought their meal.

Before she left, she said, "I'm sorry about what happened just now. Of course, the manager says the meal is on the house. It's not often we get famous people in here. You are an amazing cricketer."

It felt strange hearing her use the word "are."

His cricket days were long behind him, but he could still appreciate the fact that she still remembered him as the cricketer he was.

They ate their meal in silence, since they both had things on their minds.

When he was done, he placed his fork on the plate and leaned back in his chair.

He felt somehow alive and refreshed, almost as if he'd placed whatever burden he'd been carrying on the floor. However, now he needed to get back to the hospital. Jared would be expecting them.

As they were leaving the restaurant, his hand on Tamara's elbow, he heard the sound of people clapping. What was going on? Then he realized they were clapping for him.

Something deep inside gripped his stomach. He didn't know what it was, but there was something special about the hands that lauded him.

A voice spoke. "Mr. Austin, thanks for gracing us with your presence today. As manager of Tim's, I extend an invitation to you to stop by any time you want. By the time you come back we're going to have a dish named after you. Just call and we'll work out the details. Do you have a minute to do a few autographs?"

"Just a few minutes. A friend of mine is in the hospital so I can't stay long," Kyle said.

"There are just a few people here so you

won't be long. We really appreciate this," the manager said.

He was led to a chair and table and for the next few minutes he signed his name on whatever the patrons gave him. Somehow he didn't feel the trepidation he'd felt months ago at the thought of meeting the press or his fans.

When Jared woke up, it was to an empty room. For a moment he panicked, but when he felt the pain in his chest, he remembered he was in the hospital. That accounted for the starkly empty room and the white sheets. He also remembered the accident and the pain. And he remembered the visit with his mother.

He'd finally had the courage to go see her and it had been as he'd expected. He still wasn't sure if he could forgive her. Because of her lifestyle he'd been forced to live a life he didn't want. She'd loved him and his sister, but she'd been responsible for his sister's death and his being raised in foster care.

The music of Christmas came joyously through the hospital's intercom system. A local singer piped a reggae version of "Li'l Drummer Boy." The last time he'd heard that song was the day he'd stepped off the bus and seen smoke billowing from where he lived.

He'd rushed up only to see his home burning.

He had run as fast as he could, but when he'd reached the house, it had already been burned to the ground.

He'd searched all around until he'd found his mother, lying in an ambulance. She was unconscious.

When he'd asked about his sister, no one could tell him where she was. No one had seen a little girl. A few hours later, he discovered the truth. His little sister had died in the fire.

The next few weeks had been a whirlwind of activity. His mother's release from the hospital and then her arrest for neglect and his sister's death. A year later, she was being led away to prison. By the end of the trial, his mother had been painted as a drug addict who didn't care about her children.

By that time he had been placed into his group home. To this day he thanked God that the staff who worked in the home had turned out to be good people.

They'd encouraged him to strive to be the best. When he finished high school, he wondered what he'd do, where he would live. He'd had to move out and that's when he'd seen Kyle's advertisement in the newspaper.

Everything had turned out well for him.

He hoped Kyle wouldn't be angry about the car. He knew he'd let Kyle down. He'd always been so careful when he drove, remembering that the car was not his.

He'd offer to pay for the damages. He'd put off getting his doctorate and go get a job.

When Kyle came he'd be sure to tell him. He just hoped he didn't get fired.

He was beginning to feel tired again. He'd get some sleep and then speak with Kyle when he and Tamara came to visit.

When Kyle and Tamara entered the hospital room, Jared was awake and watching television.

His eyes lit up when he saw them, but he glanced over at Kyle and quickly looked away. Something was bothering him, Tamara thought.

"Hi, Jared. How're you feeling?" she asked.

"I'm doing fine. The doctor says I'll be out soon. At least I get to be out before Christmas. I didn't want to spend Christmas here. I remembered that we'll be going over to your brother's home for the holiday, Tamara. I'm so looking forward to it," he said.

"I know you are, but you're going to have to promise us you'll take things easy. Fortunately, school is out for the holidays so you don't have to worry too much about your studies," she said.

"I'm glad about that," he said. He paused. "Kyle, there is something I need to talk to you about. It's important," Jared said.

"I'll just slip out for a minute then. I'll be right back," Tamara said.

"You don't have to go, Tamara," Jared said.

"No, it's fine. I need to go to the ladies' room. You have your man-to-man talk," she said.

Jared smiled at her sheepishly. She smiled back and left.

"What's the problem, Jared?" Kyle asked.

"It's not me. I just wanted to let you know how sorry I am about the car. A truck was coming in the opposite direction. It swerved and almost struck the car. I had to try to avoid the truck and I struck the embankment," he said.

"Jared, you almost died and you think I'm worried about a car? What do you take me for?"

Jared didn't say anything. Kyle moved closer to where Jared lay.

"Let me say something important and say it for the last time so we don't go back to this," Kyle said. "When I received the call about the accident, the only thing I could think of was you. I couldn't lose you and it had nothing to do with how dependent I am on you. We may not be brothers by blood, but I thought we'd established that that's how we feel. As if we're brothers," Kyle said.

"I just didn't want to disappoint you," Jared said.

"Jared Rollins, in all the years you've worked

for me, you've never disappointed me. Maybe now is the first time. But only because you thought I'd care more about a car than you. Do you think so little of my feelings for you, Jared?"

"I'm sorry I asked that silly question," Jared said.

"And remember, you always have a home with me as long as you want it. Jared, you're family." Kyle realized that Jared was sounding all choked up. The boy was crying.

"Now, I'm not sure where you are, what part of your body is hurt, so a hug is out of the question right now," Kyle said, trying to lighten the emotion in the room.

"Okay, bro," Jared replied.

"Good. Dry those tears from your eyes and I'll do the same. Can't spoil Tamara's image of us as macho men."

"Oh, I'm sure she knows we're the sensitive, caring kind of guys," Jared said with a laugh.

"Yeah, I'm sure she knows. She doesn't miss a thing," Kyle said.

When Tamara returned, Jared was fast asleep. In the chair next to the bed, Kyle sat, his hand in Jared's.

She stared at the two men who'd become so important in her life in such a short space of time.

She was already in love with both of them. With Jared she felt a strong sisterly attachment. He was handsome and though he was just a few years younger than she was, she didn't feel that strong pull of magnetism which she experienced with Kyle.

Kyle Austin had enchanted her with his sexy voice that sent chills down her spine. Now, his devotion to Jared made him all the more appealing and admirable. She recognized the sensitivity and genuine affection he had for Jared, a boy who'd lost as much as he had and who he identified with.

Maybe life wouldn't be so bad after all.

The Kyle she saw now was far removed from the grouchy individual she'd met almost three weeks ago.

He was definitely the kind of man she could love forever.

Chapter 11

Two days before Christmas, Tamara finally made it to the mall where she preferred to shop. Kyle had wanted to come, but decided to stay at home because of the large crowds expected to be there.

She'd take him shopping sometime in the New Year when the mall would be a lot less crowded.

She'd stopped in to see Jared on her way to the south of the island. Kyle would go and visit with Shayne and the others. Her brother and Kyle had bonded well. Shayne called at least once a day to chat with his friend. Last night he'd even dropped by to spend a few hours with them, helping Tamara to decorate both houses. Kyle had insisted that his house must be decorated for Jared's return home on Christmas Eve.

Tamara headed toward the toy shop where she was to meet her sister-in-law. She'd promised Carla she'd help her pick out gifts and then they'd do lunch. She was looking forward to a little girl time.

On reflection, she realized that her everyday life was surrounded by men. At the veterinary school, she'd been one of only two women enrolled, and she'd grown up around Shayne and Russell. Now, her closest friends were Kyle and Jared. It seemed she was born to be surrounded by men.

But today she needed to spend some time with her best girlfriend, her sister-in-law Carla. Tamara was looking forward to the afternoon.

They'd planned to do some shopping, have lunch and then take in a movie. Shayne was taking Darius over to spend the afternoon with Kyle. Tamara hoped they wouldn't get into too much mischief.

Of course, Darius would keep them in line.

In the distance, just outside the toy shop as she'd said, Carla stood outside the door. Tamara never ceased to be amazed by her sister-in-law's beauty. Her brother had chosen well. Carla was one of the most beautiful women Tamara had ever known. Instead of being a travel agent, Carla could have easily graced the catwalk as a model.

Her height, her slender figure and her natural grace only emphasized that Carla was in the wrong profession, but Tamara was sure Carla would never have been happy using her beauty for hire.

She knew that Carla loved the energy and quick pace that came with running the agency she'd opened six months ago on the island. Shayne had finally convinced her to open a branch of the agency Carla owned back in Atlanta, Georgia here. Already the new business was doing well.

When Tamara reached Carla, her sister-in-law embraced her with genuine affection.

"So are we going to go to the bookstore and buy the latest Brenda Jackson and Rochelle Alers?"

"Need you ask? And I've heard that Beverly Jenkins also has one out this month."

"Girlfriend, we're going to stock up on our reads. I want the Jackson book first."

"Okay, since you're older, I'm going to show respect and let you have it first."

Carla laughed. "I'm glad you know how to respect your elders. You ready to go get those books? We have a lot of shopping to do. I can't believe I waited so long to get my gifts and I can't believe the number of people here."

"Carla, remember that for the past few years you were able to do your shopping early since you were at home with Darius. This year, you're a working woman," Tamara said.

"That's true, but I'm still glad I took the day off to spend some time with you. You're my favorite sister-in-law."

"I'm your only sister-in-law."

"Doesn't matter. If you were one of many you'd still be my favorite. You'd better follow me if we're going to get some shopping done before the movie begins."

Three hours later, an SUV filled with wrapped gifts, and hearts filled with Christmas cheer, Carla and Tamara sat to enjoy fish and chips in one of the restaurants in the food court.

"I totally enjoyed that movie. Isn't Tim Allen hilarious? I'm going to bring Darius to see it," Carla said.

"Promise me you'll let me come. I want to see it again, too," Tamara said with a laugh.

"I promise. But you're going to have to talk to me about Mr. Gorgeous first."

"Mr. Gorgeous?" Tamara feigned ignorance.

"Come off it, Tamara. You know exactly who I mean."

"Oh, you mean Kyle."

"As if you didn't know who I was talking about," Carla said.

"He is hot, isn't he?"

Carla pretended to fan herself. "He's definitely hot. If I didn't love my husband, I'd…"

"I hear you, but I'm sorry, he's already taken."

"Yeah, you couldn't take your eyes off him. I was going to offer you the guest room the last time you and Kyle visited."

"Carla, I'm not that bad," Tamara said.

"You're not? So, is he good?"

Tamara blushed, but realized it didn't make sense to deny it. "Better than good. We don't seem to be able to get enough of each other."

"That will happen. And loving the person makes the need for them even greater."

"I do love him," Tamara whispered.

"I can see that."

"But I don't know if it's the best thing. I'm not sure if I'm the best thing for him. He makes me feel alive, but at times, he makes me so angry. Sometimes I feel as if I should walk away and not look back, but the road ahead would be too long without Kyle. Sometimes I think I love him too much," she said.

"Tamara, there's no such thing as loving someone too much. You either love him or you don't. All the other baggage that comes with it determines whether a relationship with him is worth it. But both of you have to be willing to deal with that baggage," Carla said.

"I understand what you mean. Kyle is so concerned about being blind. He's convinced he can't be a good father or husband."

"I'll give you some simple advice. Don't try to change him. Let him change himself. He needs to discover what he wants out of life on his own and he's the only one who can do that."

"That's true. Maybe I've been pushing him a bit too much."

"Girl, I didn't say don't go after your man. Just let him think he's the one doing the pursuing and he'll fall right into your lap."

Tamara laughed. "It's good to get some advice from a woman of experience."

Carla smiled. "You're learning," she said. "I believe that Kyle is the one for you. I see how he acts around you. His body tenses, he trembles when you're near. And then there is that look of absolute devotion on his face when he looks toward you," Carla said.

"How did you know when you were in love with Shayne?"

"I was attracted to him from the time I met him. But the day he took Darius in his hands for the first time and he cried I knew I loved him and I wanted to spend the rest of my life with him. The romance novels we read focus on the alpha male—those strong confident men who can handle anything. Me, I don't have a problem with men like that. But underneath that cool exterior, I want a man who is passionate about life and me," Carla said.

"Kyle is like that. Underneath his disdain for Christmas, he has a heart so full of love. He's been through so much in his life it can't be easy for him to open up to anyone. Fortunately, he has reached out to me," she said. "I'm not sure he loves me, but I know he feels something for me that must be a step in the right direction."

"Don't worry, Tamara. Everything will work itself out. I know it."

"Thanks, Carla," Tamara said, glancing down at her watch. "Girlfriend, it's time we get home. I'm sure your husband is wondering where you are. Let's stop at the pizza shop and bring home a few pies. I'm sure they'll be hungry by the time we get there."

"Good idea. Let's go order them and browse a few more stores until the pizzas are ready. I need to walk off some of that meal we just ate," Carla said.

The morning before Christmas, Jared was released from the hospital.

Kyle was so eager for the boy to return home he couldn't contain his excitement. He called Tamara as soon as he woke up on Christmas Eve day. He'd slept at home the previous evening out of respect for Shayne. He refused to flaunt his relationship with Tamara in front of her brother.

Of course, Tamara had protested, but he'd been adamant. She retired early, after her brother had insisted on walking her over to her own house. Darius had fallen fast asleep and Shayne had said it was time to get his wife and son home.

He had made his way over to her house and was waiting patiently for her on the porch. When she finally came out he could smell the scent of her perfume wafting in the air.

"You ready, sweetheart?" Tamara asked. "I'm sure Jared is waiting for us to come get him."

"Yes. My cell phone went off a few minutes ago and he asked me how close we were to the hospital. Says he can't wait to get a good meal. Ms. Simpson promised to make all his favorites when she arrives," Kyle said.

"You know, I have never seen this Ms. Simpson," Tamara said.

"She comes three times a week but she slips in, does what she has to do and then she's gone. She'll be here when we return from the hospital, so you'll finally get to meet her," Kyle said.

"I look forward to it. That is if you don't mind?"

He hesitated for a moment. "I think it's a good idea," he finally said.

"So you're coming around," she said.

"Yeah, I'm coming around. I'm beginning to realize that Christmas is what we make it and not the other way around. The most important thing is re-membering Christ's birth and that it's a time for families to draw close to each other, remembering those who are less fortunate than we are," Kyle said.

"Kyle, you sound so preachy."

Kyle laughed. "Okay, I'll ease up. I have a surprise for you."

"Surprise?" Tamara asked.

"The day you and Carla went shopping, Shayne took me to do a bit of shopping, too. I bought a few gifts," Kyle said.

Tamara squealed.

"Kyle, I'm so proud of you. You didn't tell me anything. No wonder you looked so pleased when we came home."

"Darius almost gave us away. He said something about seeing the clown at the store," Kyle said.

"I did hear him say that, but then Shayne said something about a clown program on television. No wonder Darius was giggling so much," Tamara said.

Kyle laughed again, a loud, hearty sound that came from deep inside him. She'd never heard him laugh like this before and she realized how much she liked the sound.

Minutes later, she drove the car into the hospital parking lot. She was glad she had to take the lead since Kyle would do anything to get them there as soon as possible.

Under Kyle's directions—and she was impressed to see him in control—Jared was released in less than half an hour.

The drive back to the house was a quiet one. Jared had fallen asleep.

There was no conversation; instead they listened to the music of the season on the radio, each lost in their own thoughts.

Later that night, Kyle knocked on Jared's door and felt his way into the room.

"You good, bro?"

"I'm fine, Kyle. Just a bit tired. Thanks for all you've done for me. I don't know how I'm ever going to repay you."

"Jared, there's no repayment necessary. We're family. We need each other. As far as I'm concerned you're the only family I've had for a long time. Yes, we've both been told that we're part of the Knight family and to an extent we are, but you and I—we have a special bond. No one knows the rough lives we've both had. We're both survivors."

"I've told you a bit about my life and I've told you that my mother's in prison. I'd never been to see her since she was there, but I received a letter from the prison informing me she wanted to see me. I was returning from visiting her when I got in the accident."

"Is she okay?" Kyle asked.

"Yeah, she seems like a different woman. Stronger now that she's off the drugs. I don't know how she feels about what she did. In any case, her remorse won't bring my sister back, but at least it's good to know she's finally cleaned up her act."

"I'm glad she's doing better. I didn't know you had a sister."

"She was ten when my mother fell asleep and the house caught on fire. My mother was blamed for what happened and that's why she went to prison."

"Man, that's hard," Kyle said.

"It was. That's how I ended up in the system, but I'm cool with it. I think I'm moving toward forgiving her. I loved my sister, but hating my mother won't bring her back," Jared said sadly.

"That's true. Christmas seems to be having its effect on both of us. I've been thinking so much about my own life and my existence. I'm ready to move on, too," Kyle said.

"I think we both are," Jared replied.

"Well, Shayne wants to know if we'd want to come over for lunch Christmas Day and I told him that would be fine with us," Kyle said.

"No problem. I'm not for refusing free food," Jared said.

Kyle laughed.

"I like my food, but that's really not the reason

I want to go. I like being over there. It's what you said about families. They hardly knew me but they made me feel a part of theirs," Jared said.

"Yeah, I feel the same way. I did feel like I belonged there."

"So we're definitely going?"

"Wouldn't miss it for the world," Kyle said.

At that moment the clock struck midnight.

"Merry Christmas!" they shouted simultaneously.

"Well, I think it's time I get some sleep," Kyle said, "but I have something to say to you first. It's part of your Christmas gift."

"You're going to have to open yours tomorrow."

"Oh, I still have a gift that's yours for tomorrow, but this one I wanted to give you now," Kyle said.

"Okay."

"Remember when I tried to increase your salary about three months after you started working for me and you refused it? I've been placing that money in a special account over the years. I know you want to go to England or the States to finish your studies. Well, you have quite a lot of money accumulated in that account. I've made sure I never touched it so it would be yours when you were ready to work on having that 'Dr.' before your name."

"I don't know what to say, Kyle."

"Just say thanks."

"Thanks, Kyle. I won't disappoint you."

"I know you won't, Jared. There's no need to tell me that."

Kyle felt himself wrapped in the briefest of bear hugs.

When Jared broke away, Kyle said, "It's time for some sleep. I promised Tamara I'd go to church with her tomorrow. Troy will come to pick you up and bring you to the house later," Kyle said.

"Good night, Kyle."

"Good night, bro," Kyle said and left the room.

Christmas arrived in a symphony of church bells ringing across the island. Already dressed for the morning service, Tamara squirted a bit of fragrance on her skin and looked at herself in the mirror.

She was proud of what she saw. She looked good. Carla had agreed with her choice of a form-fitting blue dress. She walked slowly down the stairs, conscious of the three-inch heels she wore. They made her look taller, more feminine.

She stepped outside, the chill of the early-morning breeze making her feel alive and full of energy.

She drove over to Kyle's, parked the car and knocked on the door.

Immediately, the door swung open and Kyle

stood there, dressed in a pale grey pin-striped suit that fit him to perfection.

She tried to keep dirty thoughts from her mind, but her eyes devoured him from head to toe.

"You like what you see? I may be blind, but I know when a woman thinks I'm sexy. Didn't think I could clean up so well?"

She stood in front of him and then she tiptoed to kiss him on the lips.

"Blessed Christmas, Kyle Austin. You do clean up well, I must say. But I've always known that under that grouchy exterior there was an angel trying to be released," she said.

"I'd prefer if you didn't take it that far. There is nothing angelic about me," Kyle said.

"If you say so, but I'm sure a young man I know won't agree with you. I know he thinks you're his guardian angel," she said.

"Oh, he knows that the feeling is mutual. We had a long talk last night," Kyle said.

"That's good. I'm sure things are going to begin to flow for him."

"Are you ready to go to church? The service starts in about twenty minutes, but we can easily get there in time."

When they entered the church they were greeted by the sound of music. Tamara loved her church and though she had not been there for several months, she experienced the familiar sense of belonging. She paused to speak to a few people, introduced them to Kyle and then headed to the pew where her family usually sat. Shayne and Carla were already there. When she asked about Darius, she was told that he was in a Christmas play the children would perform during the service.

Reaching their seats, she patiently waited while Kyle sat. She'd been bowled over by his appearance. His dark mahogany complexion was set off perfectly by his grey designer suit.

A few minutes after they sat, the service began.

The highlight of the program, however, took place when Darius and a group of children did a short dramatization of the manger scene. Of course, Darius was the star of the show. In his donkey costume he brayed the loudest and had the congregation in stitches.

The pastor's message was a simple one on the significance of the birth of Christ, and the fact that Christmas should be a celebration of that birth. Of course, he emphasized the importance of family and the fact that it should be all about giving as Christ had given to mankind.

At the end of the message, Tamara was conscious of Kyle's pensive mood and she knew he was reflecting on what the pastor had said.

After the service, the pastor came over.

"Tamara, I just want to wish you a blessed Christmas and introduce myself to Mr. Austin. I recognized his face and wanted to let him know he's one of my favorite cricketers even though he doesn't play anymore. I was sorry to hear about your accident," the pastor said.

"That's fine, Pastor. That was over five years ago and I've finally come to terms with my blindness," Kyle said.

"That's good, my son. God takes care of us, whatever the circumstance. You might not know that I wear a hearing aid. I'm deaf in one ear, but I've allowed God to use me in a tremendous way. My handicap has become not only a reminder of my own frailty but also a symbol of my strength," he said.

"I did enjoy your message. I was convinced you were speaking directly to me," Kyle said.

"But I was. When God gives me a message, he knows that everyone here needs it, but it will speak stronger to some than others. Again, I must say how honored I was to have you in church today. You must come and visit us again." And to Tamara the pastor said, "Please make sure you don't stay away so long. We miss you."

"I won't. And I'll even make sure I bring Kyle back with me," Tamara promised.

"Good, I look forward to seeing more of both of you. Enjoy the rest of the season." With that he walked away, his eyes carrying the happy twinkle with which he greeted all of his parishioners.

On the drive home, Kyle remained quiet and reflective.

"So you go to church there?" he finally asked, breaking the silence.

"Yes, I do. Although I haven't been often in the past few years because I was overseas studying. I just haven't had the time to come since I returned, but I plan to rectify that," Tamara said.

"I'll be glad to come with you. Your pastor seems really nice and blessed."

"He is. He helped me a lot when my parents died. Russell had Shayne to talk to and Gladys tried her best with me, but they only reminded me more of my parents. Pastor Husbands and his wife were the best people to help me."

"I'm glad you had someone to help you when your parents died. I wasn't that fortunate," Kyle said.

"What happened, Kyle?"

"After my mother died, I went to live with an uncle, but his wife didn't bank on having an extra child in her perfect family, so eventually my uncle placed me in the system. I was fortunate to find a good foster home. By the time I finished school, I was playing for the West Indian cricket team."

"You've done well for yourself," Tamara said.

"Yeah, I think I have done well. But I've changed a lot in the past few weeks and I have you to thank for that."

"Not me. You made the change. I may have been the catalyst but the changes had to come from you."

"Well, whoever, whatever, I'm glad I met you," Kyle said.

Tamara pulled into the driveway of the Knight Plantation.

"We're here, and Shayne and everybody else have already arrived. Russell was supposed to be here since last night, but his flight was delayed. I hope he gets here soon."

"I don't know if you're like me, but I could eat a horse," Kyle said.

"My sentiments exactly. But don't worry, I'm sure that Gladys and Carla have cooked up a storm."

Kyle smiled. He was sure he'd have a great meal, but he was more excited about spending the day with Tamara's family.

Several hours later, Kyle couldn't eat another bite. He'd burped softly, hoping no one would hear and stretched out on the couch next to Tamara. He was aware of her arm around his shoulders.

He heard a childish giggle and realized Darius had heard.

"Uncle Kyle," the boy said, trying to stifle his laughter. "Mommy always says that a burp means that you enjoyed the food."

"What she says is true. That's the best meal I've had in years," Kyle said.

"I'm glad you enjoyed it," Carla said. "Gladys here is beaming all over her face."

"So are you, Carla," Gladys, the Knights' former housekeeper, said. "Kyle, thanks for the compliment. Carla and I spent all last night cooking. I only had to finish this morning while you were all at church."

"And you did the cheesecake? I'm partial to cheesecake with raspberry topping. I'd marry a woman who makes cheesecake like that without hesitation," Kyle said.

"Auntie Tamara made it. Uncle Kyle, are you going to marry her and have babies?"

Kyle didn't know what to say, but he covered his embarrassment smoothly and said, "I'm sure your Aunty Tamara won't marry someone who wants to marry her just for cheesecake." He would have loved to see Tamara's expression.

"Yeah, but she'll marry you because she's your girlfriend," the little boy said.

"Darius," Carla said, "I think it's about time you stop tormenting Kyle."

"I'm sorry, Uncle Kyle."

"It's okay, Darius. I'm not embarrassed at all, but can we please change the conversation?"

The night wind blew gently on the patio where Tamara and Kyle sat wrapped in each other's arms.

"I hope you weren't embarrassed by what Darius said today," Tamara said.

"Were you?" Kyle's tone was serious.

"No."

"So why should I be?" he asked.

"I just wondered…" Tamara said. "Would you really marry a woman who made great cheesecake?"

"In a flash. Especially if she was beautiful, loved strays and knew how to take care of her man," he teased.

"I wonder if I know anyone with those qualifications. I can think of one such person."

"Can you? I'm so sorry, but I'm already taken. And I'd love this particular woman even if she couldn't make cheesecake," he said.

Tamara watched as he looked at her. For the briefest of moments she swore he could see her.

"How'd you like to spend the rest of your life with me, Tamara Knight?"

"Are you sure about this, Kyle?"

"As sure as the ring I have here in my hand," he said.

She looked at the tiny box he'd taken from his pocket. She had not expected this.

"So, will you marry me?"

"I'd love to marry you, Kyle," Tamara said with joy in her heart.

"Good, so we're official? I'm going to have to call Shayne in the morning and let him know you agreed. He's already given me his blessing," Kyle said.

"It was mighty presumptuous of you to speak to Shayne," she said teasingly.

"No, I just wanted to do things the right way. You deserve only the best," Kyle said.

"No, you deserve the best. I hope I can live up to your expectations. I'm not going to be the easiest person to live with," Tamara said.

"Oh, I'm sure that I'm not going to be the easiest person to live with either. So maybe we'll just cancel each other out," he said with a laugh.

"I'll marry you on one condition," she said.

"What's that?"

"That Jared continues to live with us."

"Of course, Jared and I are a package deal. He's grown so much, but I know there is still a lot of pain he's dealing with. He only just told me what happened on the day he got into the accident. He went to visit his mother in prison."

"No wonder he seemed so worried and distracted."

"Jared hasn't had an easy life. I'm glad I'm able to give him a home. I plan to ask him if he'd allow me to be his legal guardian. I want to make sure he's taken care of in the event anything happens to me," Kyle said.

"Nothing will happen to you. I plan to have a long life together with you."

"God willing."

"I love you, Kyle Austin."

"Show me how much."

"Your wish is my command," Tamara said with a smile.

When Tamara's lips touched him, Kyle shuddered. After all the times they'd made love, his response to her was as intense as it had been the first time.

He had no doubt that twenty years from now his response would be no different.

And he had every intention of loving her for the rest of their lives.

Tamara's mouth covered one of his nipples and he realized that this was not the time for reflecting.

This was the time for loving.

Epilogue

Tamara watched as her husband came toward her, led by Alex. The Seeing Eye dog had completed his training three months before and was now Kyle's constant companion.

She smiled. So much had changed in the past few months. This Christmas would be another wonderful one, because she had all the people she loved around her.

She touched her stomach, feeling the warmth of the life growing there. She'd tell Kyle tonight. It'd be the perfect Christmas present.

Kyle stopped for a while and she watched as he and Jared spoke. Jared was now an official

member of the family and they'd taken on the responsibility of being his legal guardians.

He'd completed his master's degree in July and
was now in his first semester as a doctoral candidate at a university in the United States. He, like
Russell, was home for Christmas.

She watched Kyle and Jared and felt an overwhelming love for them. Beyond her family there
were no two persons she loved more.

Kyle had changed, too. Of course, he'd had to
live with his notoriety for the first few months when
the news hit that he was the bestselling author K.C.
Austin. He'd agreed to a few interviews, but fortunately for the past few months his routine had
returned to normal and he was now working on his
third book. Book two had been released in early
July to phenomenal success, but he'd taken it in
stride.

Of course, this year he'd embraced Christmas
with the fervor and energy of a little boy. Together
with Jared, they'd put the Christmas tree up and
decorated the house.

She felt that familiar ache. She wished he could
see the wonderful work they did, but she knew
that now Kyle only felt the occasional regret about
his blindness. Now he lived his life to the fullest
and she made sure he did. They ran, swam, rode,
danced and made love.

Yes, she knew that the upcoming child would initially be a challenge, but as with all challenges they would learn to adapt. She had no doubt that Kyle would be a good father.

In the other corner, she glanced over at Shayne, George and Troy. Her husband's best friends. Lord, she was always scared when her husband went out with those three, but she knew nothing would go wrong.

The trio was good for her husband. Whenever he came home after a night out with the boys, he always returned energized and she thanked God each day that they embraced him despite his disability.

Of course, they didn't consider it a disability. They just considered it a special part of who he was. It made him unique.

Tamara felt the slight sting of tears.

"You alright?" a voice said. It was Carla.

"Oh, I'm fine."

"So when are you going to tell him?"

Tamara turned to her sister-in-law. How did she know? Why was she surprised? After all, Carla was a woman and her best friend.

"I plan to tell him tonight," Tamara said.

"I'm happy for both of you."

"I know. Of course, with you being the mother of two, I'm going to need as much advice from you as possible," Tamara said.

"No fear, little sister, I'm here to offer any advice I can. I'm sure Shayne will be happy to have his first nephew."

At the same time, Darius raced over to his mother.

"Mommy, can we open our gifts soon? I'm dying to open mine."

"In fifteen minutes, Darius. We wanted to wait for Uncle Russell," Carla said.

"Okay," he replied, and he was gone again.

"He's beautiful," Tamara said. "So is Andrew. Is he asleep already?"

"Yeah, at six months he still loves to sleep. I just put him down in his crib. And your baby will be beautiful, too. He's sure to have the Knight handsomeness," Carla assured Tamara.

"Well, let's go join the others. It's time to go in to dinner. Russell just arrived and went outside to see Gladys."

"I didn't realize he had arrived."

"Yeah, a few minutes ago."

"Oh, I forgot the two of you have that twin thing. Maybe you'll have twins, too," Carla teased.

"I sure hope not. One little Austin is all I'm prepared to handle, thank you very much," Tamara said with a laugh.

That night Tamara came to Kyle as he took his clothes off and slipped into bed. His penis was erect. After almost six months of marriage, he still wanted her with every fiber in his body.

He felt the bed shift when she lay next to him, and immediately reached for her. Her lips touched his and he shivered.

He still loved to kiss her. There were times when they didn't make love, and a kiss would be enough to keep him until the next time. But he wanted more than a kiss tonight.

When her hand wrapped around him, he shuddered, his whole body pulsing with anticipation.

He didn't think he'd be much for foreplay this time around. That would have to wait until the morning, after a night full of lovemaking, he thought. Right now he wanted to take her rough and hard.

And Tamara obliged. She lay on her back and he climbed on top. He held himself poised above her, anticipating his entry. His hand reached for her womanhood, a finger entering her, finding her wet and ready.

He ached, already feeling her tightness around him.

When he did enter her, her cry made its way down his spine, thrilling him with its primitiveness. He felt like he'd come home.

When he was deep inside her, she wrapped her legs around him the way he loved and she contracted her muscles around him, almost bringing him to the end before they started. He breathed deeply and struggled to bring his body under control.

"Tamara Knight-Austin, do you know how much I love you?"

"Yes, Kyle. I do."

"Then let me show you how much," Kyle said.

"So what are you waiting for?"

He started a movement that stroked her long and hard. He wanted to please her, but knew that in doing so he would also find pleasure.

Under him, Tamara moved in time with the rhythm, drawing him deeper into her with every stroke.

He eased the pace, wanting to prevent his release as long as possible, wanting to be in her until she begged for release.

But soon her body tightened and she increased her pace. She was taking control and he followed her, enjoying being her slave.

When she cried out, he joined her with a loud shout of ecstasy. Lord, he was glad they'd moved into her house and given Jared his. That way they all had their privacy.

After their releases came whispers of love.

Later in the aftermath of the lovemaking, Kyle told his wife, "I love you."

"I love you, too," she responded, moving closer to him. "I have a Christmas gift for you."

"But you gave it to me earlier," Kyle said, puzzled.

"Yes, I did, but there is something else," Tamara said quietly.

"There is?"

"Yes," she said.

"What is it?"

"You sure you're ready for this?"

"Yeah, I'm ready," he said.

"We're pregnant."

There was silence. He had not expected this. Fear flashed before him for the briefest moment.

"A baby?"

"Yes, a baby."

"I'm going to be a daddy?"

"Yep, you're going to be a daddy," Tamara said.

She knew that his shout of joy could be heard for miles around.

Russell sat with Troy, George and Jared in the bar. They'd decided to chill for the rest of the night. Christmas was almost at an end and the happily married couples were at home doing Lord knows what.

"So two Knights are down. Russell, your turn is next," George said.

"So what about you, Troy and Jared?" Russell asked.

"No, Russell, you're destined to go next," Troy added.

"Nah, I still have a year of my internship at *The Times* before I come back home," the last Knight bachelor said.

"Will you be coming home or will you marry some American woman and stay up there?" Troy asked.

"Troy, I find it so ironic that you're the one giving me all the pressure when you got the hots for Miss America," Russell said.

"Me? Got the hots for Miss America? Who you talkin' 'bout?"

"The voluptuous Sandra, Carla's friend and business partner."

"You must be crazy. The woman hates doctors and me in particular. We can't even exist in a room together without cussing one another out," Troy said.

"Oh, that's just the sensual chemistry when you're near each other. I can feel the sparks crackling."

"Oh, it's just a matter of time before you're gone. It seems that each of the Knights are going down. You all were born for love and marriage. And I say, once a Knight, always a Knight."

* * * * *

*Turn the page for an excerpt from the
explosive first episode of the passion-filled*
KNIGHT FAMILY TRILOGY
ONE GENTLE KNIGHT
By Wayne Jordan

Chapter 1

She was in paradise. Carla Nevins never ceased to be amazed by the beauty of Barbados. Her best friend, Sandra, had frequently told her about the island, but it was only after making her first trip to the island several years ago that Carla had finally understood what Sandra meant when she said after her trips that she'd been to heaven and back.

Barbados was surely heaven on earth.

In the distance, the Atlantic beckoned, its frisky waves crashing onto the beach. The sun's rays, no longer the blistering white of the day, were now a clear gold that gently caressed and warmed her. The first signs of dusk and the tropical sunset that she found awesome were already making themselves evident with the palest of oranges and yellows splashed lightly across the sky. She'd spent most of her day down on the beach, and knew it was time to take a shower and prepare for the long restless night ahead. Since she'd arrived on the island, she'd partied every night into the wee hours of the morning. The guests and locals who frequented the night-club at the hotel were a wild and friendly bunch. Like them, she had totally immersed herself in the rhythm of Barbados' nightlife.

She didn't mind losing herself in the island's pulsating rhythm. As a matter of fact, she preferred it that way. Anything to block out the nightmares that still haunted her. Now, on the island, when she collapsed on the bed in the early hours of the morning, she was too tired to dream. Her memories seemed at rest…at least for the time being.

Carla lifted the book on her lap and, for the ump-teenth time, reread the first paragraph. Frustrated, she put it back. This paper fantasy wasn't what she wanted or needed. She wanted to see him again. The man she'd seen at the reception last night.

The man whose image now remained etched in her mind.

Squeals of delight from children in the water interrupted her musings. Again, her eyes skimmed the beach, wondering if he'd ever appear. She slowly looked to the left, then to the right, and then doubled back to the bar just beyond the tennis courts.

It was him.

He stood there, looking as bored and indifferent as he had the night before. He looked in her direction, and their eyes met, touched and lingered. Although she was a distance away she knew what she'd seen in his eyes.

The same smothering awareness she'd seen the night before.

She was reminded of a performance she'd seen of Shakespeare's *Romeo and Juliet*. In that moment when the two protagonists had become aware of each other across the crowded ballroom, they had experienced something profoundly magical.

Last night when she'd seen the handsome stranger for the first time, she'd felt the magic. All night, there'd been this acute awareness, as if they both knew that the path destiny would take was inevitable. She'd been glad that she'd gone to the party.

When she'd read one of the colorful announcements that hung like Christmas decorations all around the grounds, she'd been tempted. The party with its promised local dishes, and, of course, the famous lethal rum she'd heard several of the guests talk so much about, had beckoned her. So, last night, Carla had stood sipping her glass of rum punch and wondering why she was suddenly feeling strangely light-headed and surprisingly happy.

And then he'd walked in…and her heart had stopped.

He was tall and muscular and also quite handsome. Not in the classic way, but a rugged, sun-kissed way.

And he oozed sex appeal.

Pulse-pounding sex appeal.

Carla saw it in the way he carried himself, the way his broad shoulders swayed when he swaggered and in his intense gaze.

She'd watched him for the whole night, her eyes devouring every inch of him. And she knew he was just as aware of her. Yet neither of them had made the first move.

She wanted him.

In the early hours of the morning, back in her room, she lay in bed alone, her body betraying her as she ached for a man she didn't even know.

She'd imagined him naked, his strong legs wrapped around her waist. She'd placed the pillow between her legs, hoping to stem the ache that had slowly but sweetly reminded her that she was still a woman. It had been so long.

Richard came to mind, as vivid and clear as he often had in the years since his death, and for a moment she once again felt the overwhelming grief that always seemed to consume her, threatening to take her to the brink of madness.

Carla would never forget the accident that had taken her husband, Richard, and their unborn child from her. She'd been seven months pregnant when Richard died. And when she'd held her stillborn daughter in her arms, she'd cried because she knew her last physical link with her husband was also dead. She'd wanted to die with him. At night, when the dreams came, she still did.

She closed her eyes, wanting to remember the feel of Richard's hands on her body. Despair filled her when she realized that his presence and his touch were fading.

She opened her eyes.

The man was gone.

Carla had hoped that he would come in her direction. Maybe she should have made the first move. She'd probably missed out on her chance to have…

Sex!

That was what she needed.

Her best friend Sandra had told her that much. "What you need, girl, is some hot, dirty, scream-out-loud sex. Maybe you'd start to live again," she'd said.

And Carla was already coming alive, thanks to her mystery man. Who was he and where was he?

Suddenly, her body tingled and the rush of

warmth to the core of her womanhood forced her to lean forward.

He was back.

Half-naked.

He wasn't wearing the skimpy trunks that most of the tourists sported, preferring the loose boxers the local boys and men wore, and a sheer cotton shirt.

She was disappointed. She'd wanted to see the evidence of his manhood, that telltale bulge that a woman's eyes always noticed.

In her dream last night, she'd imagined what he would look like. Long, thick and firm. Yes, long. She knew he'd be long. Knew, because in her wildest dream, she'd felt the thick length of him as he entered her slowly. For some reason, she knew that what she'd dreamed would become a reality.

She knew he would come to her.

And, as if hearing her, he started to walk toward her.

Shayne had to find out why the woman from the party last night kept staring at him. Not that he had a serious problem with her. Actually, he couldn't help staring at her either. As a matter of fact, the way she'd looked at him last night had given rise to a randy need he hadn't experienced since his teenage years.

He wanted sex.

Needed sex.

He started to walk toward her. More than anything he wanted to touch her. He needed to feel a willing, ripe body that he knew would respond to his. He wanted to bury himself between the supple legs of a woman who wanted uncomplicated sex just as much as he did.

He wanted a woman to help him live again, something he hadn't done since his parents' death. He'd spent the past ten years working around the clock and making sure his younger brother and sister had the love and attention they needed. He'd put his life on hold to make them happy.

He hesitated, drawing to a halt. What he was about to do almost made him turn around and head back to his hotel room. Then his gaze locked with hers, strengthening his resolve, and he continued toward her.

Last night, he'd thought long and hard about what he was about to do, and he had every intention of completing his mission.

Shayne could feel her eyes on him as he drew closer to where she reclined in a beach chair, and he wondered how she'd respond to what he was about to propose. Would she reject him? Would she think he was crazy? Actually, he wouldn't blame her if she up and ran away. He thought he was acting recklessly, too, but there was something about her that made him think she felt the same attraction he did. He knew she had experienced that same powerful awareness last night. Her silent, heated response to him had been proof enough. For some reason this woman had taken control of his mind and body.

Maybe he was a bit crazy.

In his dreams, he'd made love to her all night, and in the early hours of the morning, he'd awakened, his body covered in sweat and his manhood erect and straining for release.

Already he could feel the familiar stirring, the sweet ache of anticipation.

When he reached her, she broke eye contact, averted her eyes. Unaffected by the rebuff, he reached out to take her hand.

"Come with me." His boldness amazed him. He'd planned to introduce himself first, invite her to dinner…and then seduce her.

The flash of energy that raced through him when she placed her hand in his was sudden and unexpected. His heart stopped, and for what seemed like forever, he lost himself in a pair of the most unusual pale brown eyes he'd ever seen.

Damn, he wanted her.

"Come with me," he repeated.

He released her hand and waited until she rose from the beach chair and slipped into her sandals.

Then he turned and headed in the direction he'd come from. She fell in step beside him, her stride as urgent as his.

Minutes later, as the elevator moved upward, Shayne reached for her, his lips covering hers as he realized that he couldn't wait until they reached his room.

He needed her now.

He sipped of the sweetness she offered, her eager lips parting to accept his probing tongue. As he kissed her, his every sense seemed heightened. Her nipples pebbled against his chest, forcing a strangled groan from him.

She was so sexy, everything he'd imagined she'd be.

Instinctively, his left hand found one of her breasts. Left or right? It didn't matter. He groaned with satisfaction as his hand kneaded the already turgid point, and he felt its eager response.

In the midst of the haze that enfolded him, he heard the sharp ding of the elevator door as it opened.

Reluctantly, he pulled away from her, wanting to spare her the embarrassment of being caught making out in an elevator. No one entered, and again he reached for her hand as they stepped into the corridor.

As they entered his hotel room moments later, Shayne was conscious of the fact that what he was about to do was madness. But there was a strange rightness to what was happening between them. And he knew that this day would be forever special. He could hear his heart pounding, the tiny pulse at the curve of his jaw throbbing in time with the steady rhythm echoing throughout his body.

As the door closed behind him, he felt her hands on him, her touch firm, as she explored him, teasing every nerve in his body. His hands clenched at his sides, he placed his back against the door, letting her have her way. The door's coolness did little to stem the shimmering fire that raged uncontrollably inside.

When she reached to unbutton his shirt, he eased away from the door, helping her to take it off. Then her hands touched him again, moving across his chest until she sought the slight rise of his right nipple. She smiled, rolling it between her fingers, and then, like the whisper of the wind, her lips teased first the left, then the right nipple, before she placed it in her mouth. Like a baby, she suckled, and then she stopped and a coolness lingered there. He opened his eyes, realizing that he had closed them.

He could wait no longer.

When he entered her for the first time, Carla bit her lips to contain her response, but her lips parted, her pleasure evident in the scream of joy that escaped her lips. It was as she'd imagined. His long thickness filled her until she could feel every throbbing inch of him.

Instinctively, she wrapped her legs around his waist, drawing him even closer. When he groaned, she realized that his arousal matched hers.

"Damn, woman, you were born for me. Being inside you feels so right," he moaned. "Move with me."

And then he started a slow, tantalizing movement, stimulating the core of her womanhood until it took all her willpower not to spiral over the edge. His strokes, firm and controlled, caused every fiber in her body to tingle with awareness. In minutes, she felt the slow build of pressure and then the rush of pleasure as she shuddered with the power of her release.

For a moment, he stopped, breathing heavily. "Woman, you almost made me lose control. I don't want this to end so soon."

"No problem," she replied. "We have all night. I don't think once will be enough."

"Once will definitely not be enough," he whispered, his voice husky with desire, his mouth hovering over hers.

When he started to move again, his lips captured hers. This time, there was desperation in his movements. He stroked her hard and she reveled in the power of each thrust of his body. She joined him willingly, matching each stroke with her own. This time, his breathing was erratic, his movements less controlled, but she rode with the wave of desire.

Gripping his buttocks, Carla brought him closer, spurring him on, wanting him to join her this time. Her own release was near. With one final thrust that made her throw her head back and scream again, his body convulsed as he moaned with the power of his orgasm. Seconds later, she joined him, her body shuddering with the intensity of her release.

Exhausted, she wrapped her arms around him, pleased when he did the same thing. Her head against his chest, she listened as his heartbeat slowed and his breathing became a soft whimper.

Before she fell asleep, all she remembered thinking was that she'd been to heaven and she definitely wanted to go there again.

Shayne looked down at the naked woman sprawled on the bed before him. Damn, she was lovely, and he wanted to make love to her again. He glanced down at his penis, erect and ready, knowing that he'd make love to her again before the sun disappeared beneath the horizon.

There was a knock at the door and he quickly slipped his robe on before bending to pull the covers over Carla. Before he turned toward the door, she stirred, opened her eyes, and he saw the telltale flare of heat.

She wanted him, too.

He opened the door, taking the pizza box from the bellboy and giving him a handsome tip. Closing the door, he returned to the bed, placing the box on the nearby table.

"Want to eat on the balcony?" Shayne asked her.

She shook her head. "I'd prefer to stay here."

"My housekeeper Gladys would be appalled, but since she's not here and I'm not telling, the bed would be perfect."

Shayne quickly found two wineglasses, removed the bottle of pinot from the refrigerator and moved towards the bed.

He placed the glasses on a tray before placing the pizza box on the bed.

As he was about to sit on the bed, she raised a hand, stopping him. Her eyes shimmered with passion.

"You're going to have to take that dressing gown off. It wouldn't be fair for me to be naked and you dressed."

Shayne hesitated, but slipped the robe from his shoulders and joined her on the bed.

"Your wish is my command," he said, nodding. "As long as you can handle the consequences of your request—or should I say, order."

"Oh, I'm sure I can handle anything that comes my way." Shayne heard the promise in the huskiness of her voice.

"I'm sure you can. However, let me propose a toast," he said, raising his glass toward hers. "To hours of hot, unending sex."

He heard her sharp intake of air. He was sure that, like himself, she was aroused, but he was enjoying this verbal foreplay.

There was no touching, just the spark of awareness between them. He felt the familiar stir of arousal, feeling a brief moment of embarrassment. Somehow he felt exposed, vulnerable. He didn't even know her name. That fact only heightened his excitement.

While they drank wine and ate the pizza, there was no need for words. The drumbeat of anticipation rang in his ears.

When Shayne finished the last piece of pizza in the box, he placed his wineglass on the floor.

Then he reached for Carla, drawing her to him. Shayne lowered her upper body to the bed, allowing the momentum to take him with her. He could feel her breasts against his chest and ached to put the firm flesh between his lips.

He trailed his lips down her neck, nibbling as he journeyed south and then he paused, unable to keep his eyes off her.

When he pulled the first dusky nipple into his mouth, Carla groaned, a jarring sound that seemed to come from deep within the core of her body.

Shayne sucked and tugged, enjoying the arching of her upper body as he moved against her.

Shifting his head, he took her other nipple into his mouth, honoring it with the same attention. Underneath him, Carla moaned, her volume increasing as she gave in to the passion burning between them.

For a while he suckled, enjoying her soft sounds of pleasure. But then Shayne wanted to kiss her. He moved upward, teasing her. He grew more excited with each passing moment.

When her thighs fell open, allowing him access, he knew he wanted more of her, more from her. He wanted to feel her warm tightness around him. He wanted to know her in the most intimate way, again. When her body jerked against him, his own tensed immediately and its response to her was as powerful as the first time they made love.

He could wait no longer.

Shayne raised himself slightly above her and then plunged inside her until he felt as if he'd jumped off a cliff and now soared above the clouds.

Carla's legs wrapped around him, drawing him even farther in, and he reveled in the heat coursing through his body.

Shayne stroked her lustily, allowing his penis to

touch deep within her. The flames intensified as they moved together in the age-old dance of passion accompanied by the earthy music they made.

Too soon, he felt the fire inside flare as every muscle in his body came alive. Shayne didn't want it to end. He wanted to prolong the feeling of euphoria that only came with the ultimate climax.

Shayne felt Carla's body tense, and he gave himself over to the joy as she joined him in flight.

He felt his every muscle and nerve tighten, and then he lost control and he shuddered with the intensity of his release.

When his eyes locked with hers, he saw a look of surprise and wonder wash over her face. In that moment he knew that something strange and special had taken place between them.

Minutes later, he drew her to him, holding her gently against his chest.

When he closed his eyes, he wasn't aware of the tears that trickled down her cheek.

All he knew was that he wanted her again.

Carla stretched, sighing with utter contentment. Her body ached all over, but the weariness she felt only served to remind her of the incredible night spent with a stranger. He'd taken her to a place she'd never been to and, to be honest, she wouldn't mind going back there again.

She opened her eyes slowly, adjusting to the dimly lit room. With the thick curtains drawn, only valiant trickles of sunlight succeeded in allowing her to see the naked man stretched out beside her. Hearing gentle snoring, she turned toward him and her breath stuck in her throat. Despite the dullness of the room, she could see every chiseled ounce of his body. He lay on his stomach, his arms tucked under his pillow. Her eyes trailed the wide expanse of his back to his narrow waist and down to his firm, sculptured behind.

When she realized the snoring had been replaced by heavy breathing, her gaze moved upward and immediately locked with his. His eyes, hot flames, blazed, reflecting the same desire she knew burned in hers.

She wanted him again.

As if he'd heard her, he rolled toward her, straddling her and parting her legs in the same fluid movement. When he entered her this time, her response didn't differ. She welcomed every inch of his thickness, amazed that somehow the temporary emptiness had disappeared. With each thrust, she raised her body to meet his, wanted to join in the dance performed by centuries of lovers. Carla realized that this moment would never be enough, that, somehow, this man had totally captured her body and she'd already lost a part of her soul to him. In her mind, words of love he would not want to hear tore from her lips, but she made sure that they remained there.

Then the sweet pounding in her head started and the familiar soar of pressure sang in her ears. When the moment came, she didn't care that the walls of the room might not be thick enough. Her cries of release joined his, and all she knew was that she'd met the man of her dreams.

Shayne jumped awake as something screamed in his head. Damn, his cell phone.

He slipped from the bed, trying not to wake the woman who lay next to him.

Finding his pants in the dimly lit room proved to be difficult, but he eventually found them and pulled his phone from the pocket. Recognizing the number, he quickly flipped it open.

"Patrick, there had better be a good reason for disturbing me," he said softly. He didn't want to wake his lover. She needed her rest. Two days of unending lovemaking must have taken its toll on her.

"Sorry to disturb you, Shayne, but there's a fire in the fields to the north of the plantation," Patrick said. "The fire service has already arrived. The two families who live along the road which borders that area have lost their homes."

"I'll be there in ten minutes."

"Shayne, take your time. The only way you can get here in ten minutes is if your car can fly."

"Fifteen," he responded with a chuckle. "I'll see you in a bit." He folded the phone.

This was definitely not how he wanted his week to end, but he had to go. The fire could spread and destroy some of the sugar crop.

Quickly putting his clothes on, he slipped into his sandals, all the time watching the woman who lay asleep.

Damn, she was beautiful. Why did the fire have to happen at this time? Shayne didn't want to leave her, but he'd be back. He hoped this wouldn't take too long.

Before he left the room, he went over to where Carla lay asleep.

Bending toward her, he touched her cheek with the gentlest of kisses.

God, she was incredible. Already he was hard again with his need for her. Somehow, he didn't think he'd tire of her, and that scared him.

But he'd be back.

The drive to the site of the fire took longer than he expected. The increasing traffic in Barbados reminded him of the few things about the island that annoyed him. He loved to drive in the countryside, but going into Bridgetown was something he tried to avoid as much as possible.

At the Warrens roundabout, the car crept along inch by inch. Images of Carla were the only things keeping him from going crazy. She'd gotten under his skin, and for the briefest of moments he questioned his no-strings-attached resolve.

But his few days with his woman were only a fantasy. In a day or two, he'd be back to reality. The passion, the lovemaking, the tender touches, all were parts of a dream he was currently living.

Now, he was going back to the real world.

Going back to the loneliness.

The thought made him sad, but holding on to a glimmer of a dream was foolishness.

For now, he'd enjoy the reality of the moment. And he had every intention of enjoying every minute with his lover.

Chapter 2

When Carla woke the next time, the dream had ended as quickly as it had begun. She was alone in bed.

Her eyes immediately went to the floor. His pants and shirt, tossed there in the heat of passion, were nowhere in sight.

He was gone.

Only memories bundled in rumpled sheets and the lingering musky scent of lovemaking remained. However, she didn't need to close her eyes to conjure an image of him. He remained fixed on the slate of her mind's eye.

Carla groaned.

Her body still ached for his touch. She wondered where he'd gone. In the two days since their meeting they'd not left the hotel room. The hours of lovemaking had only been interrupted a few times to eat and sleep.

She'd hoped that in her final days on the island they would get to know each other. In their few moments of conversation, she'd only discovered his name and the fact that he owned a large plantation on the island. Beyond that, there was very little she knew about Shayne Knight.

During their lovemaking she'd sensed his loneliness and desperation. Despite his attempt to remain untouched by unexpected feelings and his effort to maintain an emotional distance, Carla realized that, like her, he was losing.

At moments when he believed her to be asleep, she'd felt the whisper of a kiss or the gentleness of a caress. Most of all, she could not fail to respond whenever he wrapped his arms around her and she embraced his sad emptiness. Her own emptiness could not help but respond.

Troubled, Carla slipped from the bed, allowing the sheet around her to fall to the floor. The chill of the air caressed her still-heated body and her nipples tightened. She reached for her robe and a sheet of paper floated to the floor. She hesitated, dreading the message she knew would be there.

Or maybe it was a note telling her he would be back.

Carla bent, slowly picked the note up and placed it on the bedside table. After her shower, she would read it, but now, she wanted to wash the lingering warmth from her body. She headed to the bathroom but turned abruptly.

She couldn't wait. She had to read the note now. She picked it up again, unfolded it, her hands trembling.

The message was simple.

Had a great time. Have to return home to deal with an emergency. Shayne.

That was it?

No telephone number? No "I'll see you later"?

Why was she disappointed? Isn't that what they'd agreed to?

No strings attached.

Yes, that had been the agreement. But somehow she thought the time spent together had meant something. That somehow he'd been moved by the incredible lovemaking as much as she had been.

At first, what they had taken part in had been sex as primitive and unemotional as two strangers might expect to experience. But something had happened as the clock slowly ticked the hours away. The feelings had changed; the kissing and touching had become more than physical manifestations.

Her soul had become involved.

Her heart had been touched.

Carla felt a profound melancholy. The fact that he'd left without knowing how to contact her meant that, unlike her, he was unwilling to reach out for more.

Despite the glimpse of forever, he'd walked away. No strings attached.

Carla stepped in the shower and turned it on. The sharp sting of cold water shocked her momentarily, but she refused to adjust the temperature. She needed something to return her to reality.

For two days she'd allowed herself to live in a fantasy world of romance and happily ever after, hoping that somehow her knight in shining armor would declare his love for her and take her away to his castle, where they would fall deeper in love.

When the tears came, Carla was not surprised. She'd expected them. She knew that she needed to purge the rejection and sense of loss.

Minutes later, when she stepped out of the shower, she'd returned to being Carla Nevins, owner and director of a chain of travel agencies in Arlington, Virginia.

Widowed…and with no intention of marrying again.

No strings attached.

She needed to keep her resolve to remain single in focus. She'd allowed a silly holiday romance to tempt her from the straight road she'd mapped out for her life.

Losing her husband and child had devastated her and she'd vowed never to love anyone so much again. And here she was, after more than five years of living that vow, losing sight of the safe life she'd planned for herself.

Feeling like singing "I'm going to wash that man right out of my hair," she stepped back into the shower, but decided against the tune; singing was definitely not one of her talents.

Today, she would go on another of the scheduled tours around the island. Though she'd visited Barbados before, there were several places she wanted to see. Many of the guests spoke highly of the tours, so maybe that would be the perfect activity for the day. She could not resist the lure of the lush Barbadian countryside.

Since her travel agency specialized in Caribbean holidays, she frequented all the islands. However, a year didn't pass without her spending a few days in Barbados, soaking up the golden sunshine on one of its many beaches.

Her shower completed, Carla returned to the bedroom, quickly put on a pair of jeans and a T-shirt with the logo of her company on it, then left the room, a wide smile on her face.

She had every intention of enjoying the rest of her stay in Barbados.

With or without Shayne Knight.

Sex changed everything...

Forbidden Temptation

ESSENCE BESTSELLING AUTHOR

Gwynne FORSTER

The morning after her sister's wedding, Ruby Lockhart finds herself in bed with her best friend, sexy ex-SEAL Luther Biggens. Luther's always been Ruby's rock...now he's her problem! She can't look at him without remembering the ways he pleasured her...or that she wants him to do it again.

THE LOCKHARTS

THREE WEDDINGS AND A REUNION
FOR FOUR SASSY SISTERS, ROMANCE CHANGES EVERYTHING!

*Available the first week of November
wherever books are sold.*

Business takes on a new flavor...

SEX ON FLAMINGO *Beach*

Part of the Flamingo Beach series

Bestselling author

MARCIA KING-GAMBLE

Rowan James's plans to open a casino next door may cost
resort manager Emilie Woodward her job. So when he asks
her out, suspicion competes with sizzling attraction. What's
he after—a no-strings fling or a competitive advantage?

"Down and Out in Flamingo Beach showcases
Marcia King-Gamble's talent for accurately
portraying life in a small town."
—*Romantic Times BOOKreviews*

*Available the first week of November
wherever books are sold.*

KIMANI™
ROMANCE

www.kimanipress.com

The stunning sequel to *The Beautiful Ones*...

feel
THE fire

NATIONAL BESTSELLING AUTHOR
ADRIANNE BYRD

Business mogul Jonas Hinton has learned to stay clear
of gorgeous women and the heartbreak they bring.
But when his younger brother starts dating sexy attorney
Toni Wright, Jonas discovers a sizzling attraction he's
never felt before. Torn between family loyalty and
overwhelming desire, can he find a way to win the
woman who could be his real-life Ms. Wright?

"Byrd proves once again that she's a wonderful storyteller."
—*Romantic Times BOOKreviews* on *The Beautiful Ones*

*Available the first week of November
wherever books are sold.*

ARABESQUE®

www.kimanipress.com

KPAB0221107

Love can be sweeter the second time around...

USA TODAY Bestselling Author

KAYLA PERRIN

Midnight **D**REAMS

Betrayed by her husband, Jade Alexander resolved
never again to trust a man with her heart. But after
meeting old flame Terrell Edmonds at a New Year's
Eve party, Jade feels her resolve weakening—
and her desire kindling.

Terrell had lost Jade by letting her marry the wrong man.
Now he must convince her that together they can make
all their New Year wishes come true...

"A fine storytelling talent."
—the *Toronto Star*

*Available the first week of November
wherever books are sold.*

ARABESQUE®

www.kimanipress.com

KPKP0251107